Ca

MW00938364

Madison Stevens

The cauldron of tension at Luna Lodge is threatening to boil over. With distrust mounting between the military and the hybrids, Cato is forced to walk a tightrope between the two factions, or risk the situation exploding into violent disaster.

His balancing act is threatened by the presence of the distractingly attractive Staff Sergeant Wendy Morris. He can't trust a woman who is with the very military oppressing his people.

Wendy has worked hard to rise in the ranks of the ultimate male-dominated field. She's not crazy about her current assignment, but if her superiors think the hybrids are a threat, then she's not going to question them. However, the more she gets to know the moody and handsome Cato, the more she starts to wonder just who the threat is.

When unexpected trouble descends on the Lodge, the pair will need to team up to keep everyone around them safe and protect their own chance at true happiness.

Copyright © 2017 Madison Stevens

ISBN-13: 978-1542464376

ISBN-10: 1542464374

Cover designed by Najla Qamber Designs

CHAPTER ONE

SOME SOLDIERS LOVED the fact that no matter where you were stationed, you could always get certain foods: burgers, fries, that sort of thing. A taste of home.

Wendy chuckled at the thought. She didn't know whether she was impressed or annoyed that her food options weren't more exotic. Somehow when she'd first arrived at Luna Lodge, she'd thought they would be.

Then again, there was no reason they should be at that moment. Even though the hybrids' land lay within US borders, dealing with the amber-eyed super-soldiers of Luna Lodge was a far stranger experience than those she'd had when stationed in the Middle East or Asia.

She sighed. None of that changed her real food issue. The burger and fries on her plate didn't do much to summon her appetite, but she knew there wasn't going to be much chance to eat as the day went on. Not to mention the banana and granola bar from breakfast would only get her so far.

Moving away from the serving line, she glanced around the dining hall. The great space, once designed to be where guests of Luna Lodge would eat, now found itself full of hulking hybrids and military personnel.

Or, if she thought about it a different way, it was filled with super-soldiers and normal soldiers. It was an odd mix for such a grand place, but that was the world she now lived in.

Across the room, Jamie and Leah waved for her to come sit down. She smiled a little. The two women had recently arrived to help with the education of the younger hybrids.

The previous teacher had gone missing a few weeks ago,

and Colonel Hall wasn't taking any chances with the hybrids selecting their own teacher again. The commander was convinced the whole thing was part of some sort of scheme by the hybrids. Instead, she brought in two who had taught at their last installation.

Wendy didn't mind. It was kind of a nice treat for her, really. There weren't that many women transferred into the unit assigned to Luna Lodge, and she was glad to have two she already knew.

She slid in next to Jamie, who was practically bouncing in her seat. Her short brown hair had flipped out to frame her shoulders and made her look about ten years younger than she was.

"You won't believe it," Jamie exclaimed.

Wendy raised a brow to Leah. They both knew their friend was more easily excited than either of them would ever be.

"What's going on?" Wendy asked and took a bite out of her burger.

Subpar. Not a good start.

"We have dates," Jamie said. She grinned from ear to ear.

Wendy nearly choked on her bland burger.

"Correction, you have a date," Leah said. "I'm just there as a bonus."

Wendy stared between the two women. "Well, that didn't take long."

"You know how they had one of the hybrids bringing the boys to class?" Jamie said.

Wendy nodded. It had been a point of contention for a bit with Colonel Hall, but things had been going smoothly as far as Wendy knew. Besides, it wasn't like they couldn't allow the hybrids to be involved in some way with the education of their own people.

"Well, the guy who picks them up is always so quiet," Jamie continued on, picking at her meal as she did so. "I was just sure he didn't even know I existed. Then suddenly he asks what we're doing this Friday. Can you believe that?"

Leah sighed loudly. "He only included me because it would have been weird."

Jamie turned and made a face. "He said there would be some other guys there. You're just mad that you can't hide away and read all weekend."

Wendy watched them in silence, chewing her food. She wasn't much for drama, and so didn't want to say something that might draw her into the argument.

Leah set her fork down on her tray to properly stare down Jamie. "And what's so wrong with staying home and reading?"

Jamie snorted. "Nothing," she said with a smile. "If all you want to do is read about hot and sticky sex instead of actually having hot and sticky sex."

Wendy sighed again. Her friend's sexual appetite rivaled many of the men she was around. She wasn't against a little fun, but Jamie always seemed to jump into things too quickly.

In the end, Jamie spent more time being hurt by her assumptions than anything else. There was a part of Wendy that wondered if her friend was going through a bit of self sabotage maybe so she never had to actually deal with a real relationship. Wendy knew more than a few women like that.

"Well, you all have fun," she said.

She was slightly surprised at first that a hybrid had shown interest in her friend, but then when she thought about it, it made sense.

Luna Lodge was the ultimate sausage party. The hybrids might be genetically engineered, but they were still men, and most of them had to be wanting women.

Leah let out a sharp laugh. "You want to talk about never getting any? You're looking at the wrong person. Surrounded by fit men in uniform, and she's still single."

Wendy looked down at her tray. She'd tried her best, but they still had drawn her in. Maybe if she pretended they weren't looking at her they would stop. She glanced up from the food and found them both watching her.

"Whatever," she said. "You don't get it because you're a civilian."

Leah frowned. "What's that have to do with it?"

"I have to work with the other soldiers in my unit. I don't want to fuck things up with a relationship."

Jamie glanced around. "Sure, sure. What about one of the hybrids?" She fanned herself for a moment. "A lot of these guys…"

It wasn't that Wendy hadn't noticed. Hell, she'd have to be blind not to see the God-like physiques of the hybrid men, but it just seemed like a bad idea. Who knew what was going to happen with them?

Plus she didn't want to have to make a choice between her duty and her boyfriend. After all, the main reason the Army was there was to keep an eye on the hybrids. She didn't feel great about that, as it seems like they were more victims than aggressors, but that call was way above the pay grade of a staff sergeant.

"I'm good," Wendy said with a smile.

Jamie rolled her eyes. "That's not what your vibrator says."

A loud choking noise came from behind her. She turned and found a corporal standing there. His face was beet red, and he was looking anywhere but at her face.

She glanced down. He wasn't holding a tray. So, this wasn't a chance encounter.

Damn it. She turned to glare at Jamie. That was the last thing she needed getting around. She liked her teacher friends, but they just didn't understand what it meant for her to be a staff sergeant in the US Army.

"Get to the point, Corporal," Wendy barked.

"Um, Colonel Hall would like to see you when you've finished," he said.

Wendy nodded and watched the man quickly run off. She was sure she'd have her friend's words come back to bite her in the ass later.

She tried so hard to avoid drama, but it still managed to drag her in. Fun, fun.

"Ugh, what does she want now?" Jamie groaned. "Can't she let you eat one meal in peace?"

Wendy shook her head. She'd heard their complaints so many times now, they didn't really upset her.

She could even understand how they saw things. Unless you served, a lot of things about the military probably seemed oppressive, even when they were necessary for good order and discipline.

"She's really not so bad," Wendy said, and took a couple bites.

"Define not so bad," Leah said. "Because I think we have different definitions."

Wendy took a drink of her soda. "She just likes things by the book, and order is important. She's a colonel in the Army. She has to be strict."

Jamie grunted. "She's a battle-ax, and her rules are only making things worse."

"You're just mad that your date has to end at ten."

Jamie huffed and shoved a bite of pasta in her mouth. Wendy could see their point, especially with grown women having to deal with a lengthy curfew.

Colonel Hall could sometimes be a bit... much, but Wendy knew how much she'd sacrificed to get to where she was. A woman in her position had to be hard, or everyone else would walk all over her.

She also knew the colonel cared. Over the last few years, she's seen the softer side of the woman and knew the impact her job had on her. She didn't just want to be the rules person, but the protector of people. It was just how she was able to best do that.

Wendy popped the last of the burger into her mouth and stood up.

"We still meeting at your place for beer?" Leah asked. "Unless Colonel Hall prohibits that, too."

"We're still meeting," Wendy said. She had a feeling she was going to need a big drink later.

CHAPTER TWO

CATO MADE HIS WAY to Titus's office. He wondered how much longer the leader of Luna Lodge would even have a space there. It seemed like everyday the military was taking over more and more. Luna Lodge was looking less like their chance at a home and more like just another military installation.

When he was feeling more cynical, he couldn't help but wonder if it was becoming something worse: an armed prison camp.

The only up side of the whole situation was that the men stationed there seemed to be okay. Sure, they had a job to do, but most of them were friendly enough. None of them seemed to hate hybrids, or at least they didn't openly show hostility.

That didn't prove anything, though. The hybrids had been through this before. When Major Carter was stationed at the Lodge, he'd been a major supporter of the hybrids. That didn't prevent some of his men from helping the Horatius Group attack the hybrids.

Hybrids had died because of traitorous human soldiers. No matter how nice they might act, he needed to keep that in mind. The only people who could really be trusted were other hybrids and their mates.

He bit back a growl. It seemed like those in the government were good at turning their backs on what happened and then sweeping it under the rug. The hybrids certainly hadn't.

They took the humiliation and violence in stride because their leader ordered them to. They trusted him. If it weren't for Titus, things could have gotten rough, and the world could have been given a true reason to fear hybrids.

As it was, most hybrids, regardless of their feelings were keeping things to themselves. Cato hoped everything would be okay, but he also suspected that eventually the military or government would push them too far. The hybrids needed to get out from under their thumb before that happened and more people on both sides died.

Cato nodded to Ava at the front desk and proceeded to knock on the door. It seemed silly as they knew in advance that he was there, but for some reason, it messed with human minds if they didn't at least follow some social norms.

Not waiting for a response, he stepped inside. He wasn't surprised to see Sol and Titus waiting for him. They each nodded a greeting.

"Thanks for stopping in," Titus said.

Cato shrugged. Since the military insisted on guarding the fence and walls, there wasn't much for him to do these days.

He couldn't complain too much, as they were, by all measures, doing a good job, including keeping out protestors from town, but it felt wrong to be sitting on his hands when everything around them was falling apart.

Not like there was much of a choice at the moment. The hybrids were waiting for the next step, even if most of them had no idea of what that might be.

Many of the men guessed that their leaders were up to something. No one pressed for information. They all knew that sometimes the best strategy was not knowing, and no one wanted to let something slip to the military that might harm the hybrids.

Cato understood that. He'd felt and thought the same way. It wasn't until a week ago that he had been brought in on just what that next step would be.

An underground bunker. Just thinking about it still blew his mind and pissed him off a little.

They were just going to take to living in tunnels under the

ground like rats? The whole idea was off-putting to him.

They'd struggled, sweated, and bled to build Luna Lodge into something. They'd fought against the hatred and prejudice, fought to prove they deserved a place in the world.

Not only that, hybrids had died for Luna Lodge.

The bunker plan would be running away from everything they'd built and sacrificed for. It would be telling the world they had ceased to exist. Even though he'd follow his leader, it didn't change the fact that this plan felt like giving up. Maybe even a little cowardly.

Running away wouldn't solve anything. Their enemies would still be out there, waiting for them when they came back above ground.

The Horatius Group wasn't about to let the hybrids continue to make a mockery of their former masters. There was no way the hybrids could wait them out.

It didn't matter what he thought. He didn't get a say in all this. He wasn't their leader, and even if he were, he didn't really have a better solution.

For all their sacrifice, they did have to consider the future. They had children to worry about and more on the way.

Then there was the other problem with sealing themselves off: Vestals, the only possible mates for hybrids.

Although the men had been steadily finding Vestals and bonding with them, the vast majority of men still lacked a mate. If they'd fled and hid, the men without Vestals would stand little chance of finding one.

No more Vestals meant no future for their people, and most of the men being doomed to live out the rest of their lives without their other halves.

It was a double-edged sword. If the hybrids sought shelter, most would never meet their Vestals, but if they stayed as they were, they would have little means to protect their Vestals.

Not that he had Vestals on the brain. Or at least, that's

what he told himself. Cato wasn't so sure that he needed a Vestal, but wasn't so sure he didn't.

It was hard not to wish for bonding after seeing his brothers so happy in love. And the longer he waited for the right time, the more certain he was that there might never be one.

He was a hybrid. Until the Horatius Group was destroyed, he had no way of guaranteeing that it would be safe to be around him.

He shook himself a little. Now wasn't the time to be thinking about that. His lack of love life had little to do with why he was there.

Cato took the seat across from Titus. Sol walked over and leaned against the desk.

"What did you need?" Cato asked.

"Kyros and his bonded have sent word through Lucan," Titus said quietly. "Things are progressing well with the building. Another few weeks, and they will be finished with the construction."

Cato nodded.

"But in the meantime, we've got to continue to exist here without surprises," Titus said. "Many of us are being watched closely. I need you to be our eyes and ears."

Cato glanced between Sol and Titus. They all knew about the guards watching many of the higher-up hybrids. Ever since the teacher, Kyros's Vestal, had left with him, things had only gotten more tense.

Colonel Hall was obsessed with the idea the hybrids were hiding something. Given that they were, they had to make sure they didn't give her any reason to lock them down further.

"Lucan is still watching the townspeople after their attempt at turning Jasmine into a mindless drone like they are," Sol said. "Things have been mostly quiet since then."

Cato frowned. "That's a good thing, right?"

Sol shrugged. "Hard to tell. They may have just gotten better at hiding their activity."

That was true. They knew the townspeople were being mind-controlled by some sort of strange government signal. Even though the hybrids could disrupt it at short ranges temporarily, whoever controlled the signal seemed to be refining it.

At first, it was just weird behavior or extreme emotions. It'd grown recently. Now they could direct victims to do all sorts of things, including attack the Lodge, without the people even seeming to be totally aware of it.

Given all that, it wasn't that crazy to think that their enemies might just change how they played the game to throw off the hybrids. The hybrid-hating Senator Woods was certainly smart enough to push for that sort of thing.

Titus nodded to Sol before returning his attention to Cato. "For now, we've closed off the tunnel under the shed."

Cato frowned. "Isn't that our best way out right now?"

Titus nodded and pressed his fingers together. "It was also their best way in, and they were the ones to make the hole."

That didn't make sense. Why would they want in? Whatever they were doing, they didn't seem to want anyone to know. Unless the military was a part of it all.

"Do you think Hall is a part of this?" Cato asked.

Titus shrugged. "We don't think so, but after what happened, it's hard to rule out. That's where you fit in. We need you to watch them. Figure out what their plan is."

"I'm not really sure I can help much with that."

After all, no one talked to him about much of anything. And he preferred it that way.

His friend Alair liked to say he was "friendly challenged." Cato didn't really see it as that way. Maybe if everyone stopped talking out of their asses, there wouldn't be a problem.

Titus gave him a reassuring smile. "No, you are just the hybrid for the job."

His smile and words didn't reassure Cato.

CHAPTER THREE

WENDY WALKED BRUSQUELY beside the colonel along the road to the main offices where the hybrids worked. The older woman, just as sure with her walk as she was with everything else in her life, strolled with ease down the road.

Wendy glanced down at her clipboard as they moved. The list of items there was easy enough to read, but that didn't give her any insight into their meaning. The items seemed very random and not related at all to the needs of their current mission.

"I'm confused," she said, and glanced over to the colonel.

Colonel Hall wasn't a woman to keep unnecessary secrets from her subordinates, but it felt like Wendy was suddenly out of the loop.

Without missing a beat, the colonel stepped out of the way of an oncoming military vehicle.

"We're having a party," she said. The utter lack of enthusiasm in her voice didn't quite match the words she'd just spoken.

That was not remotely the response Wendy had been expecting.

"Ma'am?"

Colonel Hall stopped on the other side of the road to look at her.

"Tensions are high right now," she said. "Too high. We're supposed to be here to defuse the situation, not make it worse. The hybrids don't trust us, and we don't trust them. I need to find a way to ease things, and a party is the best way I know how."

Okay. Things were getting weirder by the second.

Wendy stared at her for a moment, blinking and processing what she'd just heard. They were going from watching the hybrids like hawks to having a party?

As if reading her thoughts, the colonel continued.

"That's not to say I've forgotten about the missing school teacher," she said with a stern look. "This also has practical implications. They are up to something, and if I'm ever going to find out what that is, I've got to open the door." She shook her head. "We need to get to the bottom of this before things get out of hand and someone gets hurt."

Wendy stared at her superior. Although she might not have agreed with how things were being handled with the hybrids, she knew Colonel Hall meant well for everyone involved, even if it didn't always seem like it.

The colonel had rules and expected those rules to be followed. It was what propelled her so far in her career. If she had given just an inch at any point, the male-dominated culture she was in would have eaten her up. So she had to be tough.

Wendy also knew her to be fiercely loyal to her troops. The colonel wasn't a woman to just give an order for no reason. She didn't give a task she wasn't willing to do herself and always had an open door if someone needed to talk. More than once she'd seen the colonel go to bat for her troops, even when it might have been better for her career to use them as a scape goat.

In the end, it was that loyalty that made Wendy want to serve with her. She knew that she would always be judged on her merits and not her gender.

"Do you really think they had something to do with the teacher? She could have just as easily run off," Wendy said. "These hybrids can be pretty intense. And the protests from the town don't make it any more comfortable."

The colonel frowned, and Wendy knew she'd overstepped her bounds. Although Colonel Hall had never limited her about what she could comment on, Wendy knew there was a line. After all, it was the military.

"This party is going to be as inclusive as we can manage," she said. "That's why I've spoken with Titus to make sure we have all the help we can get."

They were clearly done talking about the teacher. The colonel couldn't have surprised Wendy more by saying that she had been talking with Titus about the party.

Colonel Hall turned and headed to the offices. Wendy scrambled to keep up. Her mind was still dazed a little by how easily the colonel had mentioned talking with Titus.

"He's got a man to help with the whole affair," Colonel Hall said. "Said he was the perfect guy for a party like this." She chuckled. "Didn't expect it from them, but maybe they have a specialty for everything. How very military of them."

Wendy followed down the hall and through the door to where the Lodge secretary was seated. She gave a small smile to Ava, but wasn't surprised when the other woman didn't return it.

Other than the new teachers, there were several other women at the Lodge, but none were very friendly with Wendy. Not that she blamed them. After all, the Army had sort of invaded their home.

Colonel Hall rapped on the door.

"Come in," Titus called.

The colonel entered, followed by Wendy.

Wendy was always a little awestruck at the sight of the hybrids up close. As much as she never wanted to admit it to Jamie or Leah, they were something else to look at. Drool-worthy even, and she had spent years surrounded by fit battle-ready men, so that was saying something.

Titus stood from behind his desk, but her gaze instantly went to the man in the chair. His dark brown hair was slightly curled and dipped just to his eyes.

She stared at him, unable to turn away from his beautiful

amber eyes. They seemed to swirl the more she stared, and for a moment, she felt herself sway hard. Wendy reached out to steady herself and closed her eyes in hopes that the dizzy spell would pass.

Large, warm hands gripped her arms as she struggled to find her footing.

Wendy opened her eyes and was surprised to find two bright amber eyes very close to her.

"Careful," the hybrid said.

His voice was low and came out as a sort of growly command. As much as she might hate herself for it later, she could feel her body respond to him. This was pathetic. Had she seriously just swooned over a hot guy?

No. It had to be something else. Maybe she'd gotten a bad bite of burger or something.

"Sergeant Morris," Colonel Hall said. "Are you unwell?"

Wendy tore her eyes from the man to glance at her superior. "Sorry," she said. "I just got a little dizzy for a moment." She turned back to the man still holding her. "Really," she said with a small smile. "I'm fine now. Thank you."

His hypnotic eyes roved over her face before he nodded and let her go. Instantly she felt the absence and wanted to throw herself back into his arms. As crazy as it sounded, it just felt right to have this stranger hold her.

Wendy swallowed. It probably wasn't a bad burger.

It was crazy. She hadn't even met this man, and she was already willing to throw herself at him. Maybe she had been spending a little too much time with her vibrator. At least Jamie and Leah hadn't been there to see it. It likely would have made Jamie's year to see Wendy swooped up by some mystery hybrid.

"I see you've picked the right man for the job," Colonel Hall said to Titus. "I think he will work quite well with Sergeant Morris on the party."

Wendy snapped her head over to the Colonel. She hadn't

realized at all that she would be the one setting this affair up. That was well outside her wheelhouse and MOS, not that she was sure what military occupational specialty covered party planning. Some sort of logistics, maybe.

"Party?" the mystery hybrid said.

Cato glared at Titus. Of course they had failed to mention that the damn mission would mean that he'd have to put together a party. That was about the last thing he wanted to do.

Putting the friendly-challenged hybrid in charge of party planning seemed about the stupidest thing he could imagine. Besides, it didn't make any sense for a reason that had nothing to do with him.

"Isn't this Hannah's thing?" he said to them.

Sol frowned at him. "She's got morning sickness and is in no shape to handle something like this," he said. "Besides, you want Lucius breathing down your neck?"

Cato frowned. The large hybrid was the last person just about anyone wanted breathing down their neck.

He glanced over to the pretty blond soldier. Several hairs had escaped her braid and framed her pink cheeks.

He felt himself harden and cursed them all. The minute she stepped into the room, his nose had told her she was a Vestal, not just any Vestal, but his own. Just when he'd gotten into a good headspace about that.

And now they wanted him to work closely with his Vestal.

What the fuck was he supposed to do? She was in the military. She was part of the very group holding his people there and subjecting them to humiliations like curfews. It'd be hilarious if the whole thing wasn't so frustrating.

"We'll hammer out some of the final details," Colonel Hall said.

He hated the way she talked, as if she had any authority over him.

Cato turned to Titus, the person he took his orders from.

Titus nodded once. "Maybe you and Sergeant Morris can talk later about how to get started."

Titus smiled at him, but he could see the underlying mission sitting right there. He needed this to happen, and Cato was a means to that end.

Titus and Sol probably already knew that Wendy Morris was a Vestal. They'd been around her enough to smell it.

Even if they hadn't expected that she would be his Vestal, every hybrid in the room could sense how they were reacting to each other. Titus had probably already put the pieces together. If anything, he was probably happy at the "luck."

Cato sighed and nodded. He turned back to the woman and groaned inwardly.

Nothing like torturing himself for the next couple weeks. Sounded like loads of fun.

"I have some stuff to take care of, but I'll be in touch soon," he mumbled.

As quickly as he could, he fled from the room, glad to have a small break before the real hell began.

He'd wait a little bit, then stop by Wendy's house to see what he needed to do. He hoped that wouldn't be too much trouble.

CHAPTER FOUR

WENDY SIGHED as she entered the little house that had been provided to her.

She was one of the lucky few to get her own place. Although if she'd known Jamie and Leah were going to show up, she might have just pushed to stay in the women's dorms. Though she suspected Colonel Hall wouldn't have liked the idea of civilians mixing so much with active duty who weren't relatives.

In any event, it was nice having a quiet place to go at the end of the day.

It was a small house. A simple living area, small kitchen, bedroom with adjoining bath. Not the sort of place you entertained people, but still a nice space. Much bigger than the place at her last assignment, which was basically a glorified tent she shared with another woman who snored loudly.

She unlaced and removed her boots and dropped her keys on the little table by the door.

Wendy walked right into the bedroom and grabbed a pair of black yoga pants and gray tank to replace her uniform. That was always the first thing she did every day when she got home.

Carefully she pulled the bobby pins from her hair and watched as all the little flyaway pieces popped out. It was always so important that she have her hair pulled perfectly back, but her hair never seemed to agree.

Wendy pulled the band off the end of her braid and worked out the French braid she'd done that morning. Instantly, her head seemed lighter with the strands not being pulled so tightly against her head.

She rubbed her scalp a little, enjoying the feeling and then shook her head. In the mirror, she watched as the now crimped hair bounced around.

She smiled. It was a wavy mess, but she wasn't trying to impress anyone, and she wasn't in uniform and so didn't need to keep things within regulation. The girls didn't give a crap how her hair looked as long as the beers were on her.

A chuckle escaped her mouth as she made her way into the kitchen, now far more comfortable.

To be honest, she would gladly buy the beers if that meant she didn't have to go to the Enlisted Club, or the E-Club as they liked to call it.

The makeshift bar was fine enough, but it was always loud, and since there were so few women there, it always seemed like they were being watched. Likely because they typically were actually being watched. Jamie was never one not to make herself known.

Wendy sighed. Nothing she could do about it. That was just how Jamie was.

She opened the fridge and pulled out things to throw together a sandwich. She'd need to eat something somewhat substantial before the girls got there.

She slapped together a sandwich. She took a large bite and hadn't even finished chewing when a knock came at the door.

She groaned a little. They couldn't have waited ten more minutes? She didn't want to go drinking on an empty stomach.

"Coming," she said with her mouth still full of food.

Wendy made her way to the door, sandwich in hand. She pulled the door open.

"I thought we said—" she mumbled around her food.

She stopped midsentence and struggled to swallow the food in her mouth.

Cato stood on the other side of the door, staring at her

like she'd just lost her mind. And to be honest, that wasn't that far off from the truth.

Wendy finished swallowing her food.

"I…. my… what?" she said, desperately trying not to stare, but failing.

She couldn't seem to make her brain think. This very large and handsome man was just staring at her and waiting for something, and she had no idea what the hell to even say to him.

Cato ran a hand through his hair, and she couldn't help but wonder just how soft it was. It certainly looked like it was soft with the way the curls fell back against his head.

"I just came by to see if there was anything I needed to start on," he said.

She frowned. "Start on?" What the heck was he talking about?

He frowned slightly. "With the party?"

Everything clicked in her head, and she felt a wave of heat as it rushed to her cheeks.

The party. He was there about the stupid party. She'd totally forgotten about it already. She still wasn't even sure why the colonel felt she should be handling the stupid thing, but orders were orders.

For some reason, she felt a pang of irritation over Cato being there to talk about the party. Of course, it was silly to think he would be there for her. After all, they had just met and were assigned to the same task, but still the irritation was there.

She was a big girl. She knew that just because she'd experienced lust at first sight didn't mean he did. She needed to just focus on her task for now and not worry about personal crap.

Wendy waved the hand still holding her sandwich toward the living room. "Would you like to come inside?"

She could see his eyes as they followed the sandwich. Her

cheeks burned even more. So not cool.

"I didn't know you were busy," he said. "I don't want to interrupt."

He glanced around a few times, almost as if trying to decide whether he should just run or not. She didn't know whether to be embarrassed or amused.

"You wouldn't be interrupting."

As she said it, Wendy could feel the shift in her voice. Suddenly, she was using a husky voice.

Holy shit. She was flirting with him! What was worse was that she couldn't even seem to stop herself from doing it. Instantly, she could see that Cato felt the shift as well.

The gaze from his hot amber eyes trailed down her body and then back up to her face. For a moment, she was fairly certain there was some sort of electric current running between the two of them. A soft hum filled her body and seemed to set every part of her on fire.

Apparently, the lust at first sight went both ways.

He stepped forward. As they stared at one another, she licked her lips.

She had no idea what was happening. One second, she was just admiring a man she'd barely met, and now she wanted to kiss him.

His gaze dropped to her mouth. "I don't—"

Someone cleared their voice behind him, and Cato stepped back quickly.

"So, should we come back later?" Leah said from behind Cato.

Wendy's cheeks now burned even more. The heat radiated up into her ears.

Cato cleared his throat. "Maybe I'll just meet you at the hall tomorrow morning. And we can go over stuff."

She swallowed, not really trusting her own voice at the moment. She nodded.

Cato stared at her for a moment longer before turning to

Jamie and Leah with a quick nod and jogging off.

"Wow," Jamie said softly. "That was so hot, I think I got second-hand orgasms."

Wendy's friend's words shoved her hard back into reality.

"Way to kill the vibe," Leah said as she stepped past Jamie into the house.

Jamie snorted loudly and stepped inside. "Whatever. I wasn't the one that opened my big mouth."

Leah sat down on the couch and folded her arms. "And what exactly was your plan? Stand there waiting until morning?"

Jamie shrugged and tossed herself onto the couch as well.

"I was hoping to see a little action," she said with a grin.

Wendy rubbed a hand against her brow. She wasn't exactly certain what had just happened, but there was no way there was going to be action.

Maybe.

Well, probably.

She hoped at least.

Never in her life had she felt an attraction like that. It was such a strange feeling. And if she was being totally honest, she wasn't sure what she would have done if Cato had made a move. There was something about him that pulled her in. Maybe there was a lot of things she would have done, and she should have been glad her friends showed up when they did.

It was silly. She had just met the man not but hours before, and already she wanted to roll around in bed with him. Sure, he was a handsome hybrid, but she'd been around many of the hybrids and never felt that kind of burning longing.

Wendy turned to the two women on the couch. They both watched her, eager expressions on their faces, clearly waiting for her to dish.

"It was nothing," Wendy said, and took a big bite of her sandwich. "He just stopped by to talk about a party we've been assigned to work on."

Leah raised a brow. "Didn't look like nothing."

Wendy stared down the other woman. She clearly wasn't letting this go.

"Wait, party?" Jamie said.

She gave herself a little mental fist bump that Jamie took the bait. If she could count on anyone to change the subject, it would be Jamie.

"The colonel wants to boost morale and create bonds," Wendy said. "Thinks a party is the way to go."

Jamie frowned a little. "And you're setting up this party?"

Wendy could hear the apprehension in her voice, and it irritated her. "So?"

Leah was the one to chime in this time. "Well, you aren't exactly known as the partying sort." She shrugged. "Not that I'm one to talk."

Wendy took another bite and sighed.

Leah was right. The colonel assigning her to this was a chance, and she had no clue what she was doing.

"So help me out." Wendy pulled out a pad of paper and tossed it over to the two. "Write down some ideas that I can use." She shrugged. "And you can tell me a bit more about the guys you are going out with Friday."

Jamie grinned. "I can do that."

CHAPTER FIVE

CATO WASN'T SURE what he had been thinking the day before. All he'd planned to do was stop by and see what he needed to do for the party. When she'd opened the door looking far less starched than when he'd seen her earlier, something in him felt the call of his inner beast.

No matter how inconvenient it might be, the cold, hard fact was that she was his Vestal. He knew it wouldn't do any good to complain to Titus. He wondered if Titus realized already that she was Cato's Vestal.

When he saw how she reacted to his presence though, he wasn't thinking about Titus, or spying, or any crap like that. He just wanted her.

Cato grunted as he made his way over to the ball room. Of all the stupid times for him to meet his mate, of course it would be now. Right when things were about as uncertain as they could get. And what the hell was his plan if he had gotten her to bed?

The lower half of him jumped at the idea of sliding into her. He stifled the growl that wanted to come out.

He was fucked. And not in the way that his lower half wanted to be. No, this was full-on trouble and worst of all, there was no way to avoid any of it. Titus had asked him to work with her and be his ears. Now there he was, facing down his only chance at happiness and not able to act on it without losing any chance of keeping his head clear.

This was a living hell. And it was only going to get worse. He would almost rather take on a room full of Glycons.

Cato stopped outside the large door and breathed in deeply. He could already tell she was there waiting for him.

Her soft cinnamon scent floated in the air around him, luring him into focusing on her.

His.

He could feel it to the very center of his being. She was his.

Cato let out the air he had been holding in and shook himself. No. He needed to keep control.

It was not like he could walk up to some soldier and give her a line about how they were destined to be together. He could only imagine how Colonel Hall would react once she heard that.

He could do this. Just walk in, get whatever he needed to do done, and go home. Sure, he might have to relieve some pressure himself once he got home, but he could fucking do this.

There wasn't a choice. He had to do this. For the sake of the hybrids.

With more force than he intended, Cato tossed opened the door. Inside he was surprised to find that Wendy wasn't alone.

"What the hell is she doing here?" he asked, his voice almost a growl.

The two women sat in some nice armchairs from the corner of the room, which they had pulled over to the middle. Wendy, in uniform, and someone he was shocked to see: Jill Hope. A cameraman stood behind them, his camera over his shoulder.

Just thinking the name Jill Hope still pissed him off. The reporter had been a pain in their ass since they were exposed to the world. The woman had been kidnapped along with Lena, the Vestal mate of Varius, when Reverend John had hatched a vicious plan against the hybrids.

The crazy bastard had intended to burn Lena alive on television, and needed Jill Hope and her cameraman there to report on it.

None of the hybrids blamed Varius for killing the bastard, but the death being televised live hadn't helped them at all in the public eye. The humans all seemed to focus on John being killed, rather than the fact the monster had intended to murder a woman.

Sure, Jill Hope had been fighting on the hybrids' side ever since, but in Cato's eyes, that didn't make up for the damage that she had done. Her reporting was half the reason so many people distrusted the hybrids.

And he didn't give a shit if she was a Vestal, something they hadn't realized until the dust settled. Almost no hybrids ever had direct contact with her, and Varius had been around his own Vestal and so focused when he encountered her that he didn't initially realize it.

Cato didn't care. It changed nothing.

"Jill Hope," the reporter said, and stepped over to where he was.

All the while Cato stared down Wendy. Was she the one who'd brought Jill Hope in?

Jill stuck out her hand, and he ignored it. The woman only smiled a little wider. Her teeth were white, almost unnaturally so. He wasn't sure he'd ever seen teeth so white.

"Titus wasn't wrong," Jill said, and grinned. "Your surly attitude is going to be a great sell. The female viewers will eat that up. Everyone loves a bad boy."

She gave him a little wink and then spun on her heels. Her shoulder-length straight blond hair swished as she did so.

It took him a few seconds to process what she'd said and a few more for the implications to sink in.

He was confused. Beyond confused. Titus set this up? The bastard didn't even bother to warn him.

"What?"

"Okay, let's get to work," she said. "I need you both in the chairs, and we can begin."

This was making even less sense.

"I don't understand," he said.

He looked over to Wendy who seemed to be having trouble looking him in the eyes. For a moment everything faded as he remembered just how close he had been to taking things a step too far.

All he had wanted to do was get the fuck through this day as quickly as possible. Now it had all gone to shit, and he wasn't even sure why. No one could be bothered to give him a two-minute phone call apparently.

"Now don't you worry," Jill said, and pulled him over to the chair. Cato sat because there really was no other choice. "This is a puff piece. Something fun to show how well things are going for you here. How well the military and the hybrids are getting along."

"But we aren't."

His gaze followed Wendy as the cameraman led her to the side. She still wasn't looking at him, and it was only irritating him more having the yappy reporter in his face.

The cameraman slid a finger between the buttons on Wendy's shirt and clipped a small microphone there.

The man was too close to his Vestal. Cato felt the low rumble in the back of his throat.

"Hey, big boy," Jill said. He snapped his eyes to hers and narrowed them. "Look, no going all glow-eyed on me. The public won't respond well to that."

Cato huffed loudly. "And why the fuck should I care what the public thinks?"

She rolled her eyes. "Boy, would have been nice if Titus had told me how thick you are," she said, and leaned in a little. "I'm doing this as a favor. You all need this. There are people out there that would like to see your people taken out for good. I'm here to help with that."

Help. People didn't just help for nothing in his opinion.

"And what do you get out of this?" he said, not bothering to hide the disdain in his voice.

She shrugged as she straightened the black t-shirt he was wearing and clipped a mic onto his pocket.

"I get an exclusive with the hybrids," she said. He watched as she continued to not look him in the eye.

"And?"

Jill turned her eyes to his, and he could finally see honesty there.

She shrugged. "And a chance to make amends. I owe Varius."

He gave a little nod and turned away. Maybe he had been too quick to judge. He was still annoyed, but she could work off her debt.

"Okay," Jill said, and stood. She frowned down at him a little. "Is that the best shirt you have?" She sighed, then shook her head. "You know what, never mind. It's very... you."

He glanced down at his shirt. What the fuck was wrong with his shirt?

"You look fine," Wendy whispered as she sat next to him.

Cato turned and was surprised to see her looking at him for the first time since he'd come in.

He couldn't help the small smile that came to his lips. Her cheeks were pink, and he loved the little strands of soft hair that floated around her face like a halo.

"Um, you just have," she said, and leaned over and slid her fingers through the front of his hair.

He breathed in deeply. The rich cinnamon scent filled every part of him and made him ache for more of her touch. If they didn't have an audience, he wasn't half sure that he wouldn't have groaned a little at the need that filled him.

When Wendy sat back, her face was even more pink than before.

"You just had a few pieces out of place," she said.

Cato swallowed. There was no way today was going quickly for him. No way in hell.

CHAPTER SIX

A SINGLE BEAD OF SWEAT TRICKLED down Wendy's back as she sat under the hot lights they had staged for the interview. The bright lights were almost blinding if she looked into them directly.

Administrative support was a long way from public relations. This sort of thing was the last job anyone should have had her doing.

Public speaking was not her forte. Hell, she had done anything she could in school to get out of speaking in front of groups. Sure, she'd had to do her fair share of briefings in her time in the Army, but those were always planned, mission-specific, and short as she could make them.

The truth was something about public speaking just made her break out in a cold sweat and filled her stomach with butterflies. Now, they wanted her to not only do that, but to do it in a situation where millions of people would be watching.

Her stomach lurched. She wondered if she'd end up going viral if she threw up on camera.

She glanced over at Cato. The hybrid remained cool and collected. It was like he did this sort of thing all the time.

She knew he didn't. At least she thought she did. Titus and a few others were the public face of Luna Lodge. From what little she'd managed to gather, Cato seemed to be a guy who didn't always play well with others, not exactly the kind of guy you'd put in front of a camera.

For that matter, he didn't seem like the kind of guy you'd put in charge of party planning, but maybe there was some sort of hybrid-specific angle she just wasn't getting.

Maybe he was just so amazing that he could flip a mental

switch and go from gruff soldier to smooth PR guy.

Wendy glanced over again at him and rubbed her fingers together. She could still feel the softness of his hair. How the waves had slipped between her fingers with ease.

She hated when guys wore too much gel in their hair. It was always stiff and made them look like a plastic doll. Not Cato though. Soft and made her wish to run her fingers through it over and over again.

She swallowed. This was not good. She couldn't let herself go down this path. If she let her guard down and got all dreamy eyed over some man, especially a hybrid, there was no telling what it would do to her career. No, she needed to stay focused.

The cameraman held up five fingers and nodded to Jill. He lowered a finger, then another.

Wendy's heart raced. It was really happening.

3... 2... 1...

"Jill Hope here, reporting from inside the mysterious Luna Lodge. I'm here to expose the inner workings of the home and sanctuary that houses the controversial hybrids that the world has only recently come to know."

Wendy watched the reporter speak into the camera with ease and wondered just what in the world Colonel Hall had been thinking. After all, there was no way this reporter was here doing this without the colonel's explicit permission. There were so many things that could go wrong, so many ways the tension might get ratcheted up by a gaffe.

Maybe the colonel hoped it'd ease the unrest down at the fence. Protests had been common, but they'd become a daily occurrence. They weren't always dignified and calm either.

For the most part, the soldiers guarding the gates and walls kept any unauthorized civilians on the outside of the walls and fence.

The fact that it was the protestors trying to break in, rather than the hybrids harassing people in town fueled more than a few uncomfortable thoughts in Wendy's mind. It was hard to know who the military was even protecting, especially when the hybrids never seemed to be the aggressors.

She knew the colonel struggled with the mission. The hybrids were in their care, and no one there wanted to see anyone hurt. Colonel Hall might be strict, but she didn't seem to have anything personally against the hybrids.

Inclusion was commonly talked about in the military. Regardless of race, religion, or gender, when you joined the service, you became a part of something bigger, after all. Maybe the military could relate to the hybrids in a way that a lot of the civilians couldn't. Even though they hadn't chosen to serve, they'd been raised as soldiers.

Wendy blinked and realized Jill was still talking. She was on live television and would need to keep her focus.

"This will be a three-part story," Jill said, "ending with the biggest event ever hosted here: a party to help celebrate the reintegration of the Army at Luna Lodge to aid the hybrids."

Wendy's ears perked up.

Three part? As in, she would be doing this three different times.

"I'm joined today by Staff Sergeant Wendy Morris and Cato of the hybrids."

Jill turned from the camera to smile at them both. Wendy responded with what she hoped was a smile, but for some reason, the muscles on her face weren't functioning quite like they should.

"I hear you two have been put in charge of party planning as representatives of your respective groups. My understanding is that you're going to come up with a party that can really help the two groups mix in a social setting."

Wendy swallowed, her mouth suddenly very dry.

"That's right," Cato said.

She sighed a little, glad that he had been there to field the question.

"Sergeant, in what ways do you think this party will be different from most?"

Wendy thought for a moment. "Well, aside from the people attending, there really shouldn't be much difference."

The corner of Jill's eye twitched a little, and Wendy knew she was going to have to elaborate.

"What I mean is that the whole point of the party is to make each side feel comfortable." She shrugged. "If we make it some big to-do or some super-formal thing, then it wouldn't really be meeting the goal."

Wendy glanced over to Cato who was watching her with interest.

"It's supposed to be fun. That's what a party is all about."

"I see." Jill nodded. "So the focus of this party is going to be more about creating an ambiance where everyone will feel welcome? What an admirable start to such a momentous affair."

Once Wendy started to think about it, the idea she'd just mentioned seemed almost impossible. Making these two groups feel comfortable around one another was going to take more than some streamers and food. It was going to take some real planning.

Shit.

It wasn't even like they had a common upbringing to draw on. The hybrids had been genetically engineered and raised in a harsh laboratory environment outside of the United States.

She only barely stopped from groaning.

Jill leaned toward her. "So, Wendy, how does your boyfriend feel about you being stationed here? I imagine it would be a bit hard considering the kind of men you're around."

She winked toward the camera, and Wendy's cheeks heated.

"I… uh… I don't have a boyfriend so that's not really a problem."

Jill raised a brow but said nothing. When Wendy looked

over to Cato, she could see him staring with interest, which only made her blush more.

"And you, Cato? Is there a special woman in your life?"

He grunted and looked away from her. She waited for his answer, but he didn't give one.

Jill pursed her lips for a second. "Well, maybe something else will blossom thanks to this party."

Wendy opened her mouth to protest, but the reporter was already turning back to the camera.

"Tune in later in the week for an exclusive look at Luna Lodge. Jill Hope, signing off."

The green light on the camera switched to red. Wendy's shoulders slumped as relief flowed through her.

"Good," Jill mumbled to herself. "New love is always a good angle."

"But…" Wendy said softly.

Jill looked up at Wendy and Cato, pinning them each in turn with her stare and a frown. "Next time I'm going to need a whole hell of a lot more from you two." She grimaced. "It was like pulling teeth. I need you to work with me a little. Remember, the point of this is PR, and you guys could have sold being together rather than running from it."

Wendy sighed.

"But we aren't together," Cato said.

Somehow his words hurt a lot more than they should have.

Jill grinned at him. "Keep telling yourself that, big guy. I'm going to get some shots around the building. I don't know what you all are planning, but this party needs to be big, memorable."

"But—" Wendy began.

"Yeah, yeah. I know you want everybody to be comfortable. I didn't say it had to be fancy, just big and memorable." Jill held up her hand. "The eyes of the nation are on Luna Lodge, and you need to make sure they see what you want them to see, because they're going to remember it."

Jill stood and strode away, her cameraman not far behind.

Cato snorted loudly as he stood. "I don't care if she's on our side now. She's still fucking annoying."

Wendy stood as well, not quite sure where to start.

Cato nodded after the reporter. "We better follow her before she causes trouble."

Wendy nodded. It was a waste of time, but she wasn't really sure she was ready to be alone with him again. She didn't trust her body's response.

"Hey you, beefy guy! How about a few quotes?" Jill shouted at some unsuspecting hybrid.

Cato and Wendy glanced over to one another and hurried outside. It was going to be an interesting time with Jill there.

CHAPTER SEVEN

THEY MISSED DINNER. Cato wasn't a fan of missing pretty much any meal, but missing his favorite hurt.

Worst of all, Cato and Wendy had followed the stupid reporter all around Luna Lodge, making sure she didn't go snooping anywhere she didn't need to be or accosting every hybrid she ran into.

The woman had a knack for asking the most wildly inappropriate questions. Even if she was supposed to be on their side now, that didn't change the fact she was annoying.

Spending all that time in a combination of tedium and irritation didn't do much for his mood. He was already over this whole damn thing, and all they'd done was one interview about the party.

By the time the reporter and her crew packed to leave, dinner time was a distant memory, and his irritation threatened to burst out.

He glanced over to where Wendy stood watching Jill Hope's van travel down the road to the main gate.

Cato opened his mouth to say something but stopped when his stomach growled loudly.

Wendy pulled out her phone and glanced at the time.

"Looks like we managed to miss dinner," she said. She chuckled. "By a lot."

"Yeah." Cato grunted. He wasn't really sure what the hell he was going to make. It wasn't like he had any skills in the kitchen at all.

"I guess it can't be helped," Wendy said with a sigh. "I've got a frozen pizza, and we still have a lot of things to work out for the party. Why don't you come over to my place?"

Cato's heart thumped in his chest. Her place?

That wasn't a good idea. Spending all day with her had been difficult enough, and at least he had his annoyance with Jill Hope to focus on and distract him from her intoxicating scent. Alone in her place, he wouldn't have a chance.

"You heard what she said," Wendy said softly. "The eyes of the nation are on us. What we are doing is more important than just a little party. It means something. So we have to take this seriously."

Cato swallowed his doubts about working together. It didn't matter how much it made him uncomfortable. She was right. They needed to make sure things came together.

Titus was counting on him to see this through. Plus, this crazy idea might actually make Colonel Hall calm down a little.

"Okay," he said.

He followed Wendy across the lot to her car and climbed in. They drove in silence around the corner to the section of the compound that was now being used to house some of the higher-ranking military personnel.

Few hybrids came near this part of the compound anymore, if only to avoid some sort of accident or confrontation that would make things worse.

Cato almost growled at the thought. This was supposed to be their home, their land, and yet they were practically prisoners.

He glanced over at Wendy. Maybe there was still a chance to stop that. Even if many in the government hated them, not everyone did. The fact Luna Lodge hadn't been burned to the ground proved that at least.

Wendy pulled in front of a small house and turned off her car. She stepped out.

Cato stepped out of the car and followed her to the door.

Inside it wasn't much different from his place. The uniform design of the houses had made it easy to put them up fast. The hybrids had planned for a future where they could live as individuals with families.

Now that future lay in doubt. It seemed like that sort of fast growth had slowed to a standstill since the military was back with them. There wasn't much point, after all, in spending a lot of time and energy building houses if they planned to leave Luna Lodge.

He still hated the idea of leaving all their hard work. So much had taken place, and despite everything, from Reverend John to Glycon attacks, this was the closest thing to a home he had ever known. The Lodge was the place they'd finally come into their own.

Cato pulled himself from the dark thoughts. It wasn't for him to decide. Right now, he had one job: party planning.

"Make yourself at home," Wendy said, and stepped into the kitchen.

He listened as she turned on the stove and then came back out carrying a beer in hand. She held it out for him.

"I'll just be a sec," she said, and nodded to her room. "I need to change out of my uniform."

He nodded and took a swig of the beer.

Cato tried to keep his mind on the party they were planning and not the fact that Wendy was changing her clothes in the other room. Thoughts of her body just made his focus turn to shit and pants uncomfortable.

After a moment she stepped out looking far more feminine than she had before. In fact, he was surprised by the pink tank and soft gray pants.

A blush sprang up on her cheeks.

"Sorry," she said quietly. "There's only so long a person can wear a uniform in a day."

When Wendy made her way to the kitchen, he couldn't stop himself from staring at her ass in the new pants. They molded to every little dip in the most perfect way he'd ever seen.

Suddenly his pants were about three sizes too small. He chugged about half the beer to help temper the rising passion growing within him. This whole Vestal thing was far more difficult than he ever thought it would be.

Wendy stood in the kitchen waiting for the pizza to cook.

There was no way in hell she could go back out there at the moment. Not with the blush she was sporting.

She didn't have to pick the pink top. In fact, she had all sorts of t-shirts she could have slipped on, but if she were being totally honest, she wanted him to see her in something feminine, wanted him to see her as a woman. Even if it was just a little.

"What are you thinking?" she whispered.

The timer went off, and she slid the pizza onto the tray and set it on the stove.

"Can I he—"

Wendy jumped at the sound of his voice so close behind her. The hand that had been holding the tray slammed into the molten hot cheese.

She winced. "Fuck."

She yanked her hand back and wiped the cheese off. Her hand throbbed. Her skin was already starting to turn bright red on the soft padding of her palm just below her thumb.

A large hand grasped her wrist and pulled it over to the sink. Cato turned on the cold water and thrust her hand into the flowing water.

"Keep it there," he said forcefully, a slight frown on his face.

She watched as he stepped over to her freezer and grabbed a few pieces of ice. He placed them in a paper towel and tied it off.

Cato stepped back over to her side. He had such large hands, but they held her wrist as if she were some delicate flower. Never in her life had she felt like she might be delicate.

He leaned in close over her hand, peering at it for a long moment. "It looks like we caught it before it bubbled up."

She stared at his face for a bit. His eyes remained focused on her battered hand.

He wasn't what she thought he was when she first saw him. Sure, he was handsome, and his hair was super soft, but he was also thoughtful, despite his surface gruffness.

She could see there was so much more going on that he didn't say as he took in the world around him. It only made her want to know more about the mysterious man.

His soft amber eyes found hers, and she felt something flutter deep in her stomach.

"Do you have any burn cream?"

She nodded. "It's in the cabinet in the bathroom."

Cato led them out of the kitchen and sat her on the couch. "You sit down, and I'll get the supplies."

Obediently she sat. When he came back into the room, he crouched down on the floor in front of her.

Cato tenderly pulled her hand into his and removed the ice. As soon as he did, she could feel the heat returning to the spot.

He dabbed on a little cream, and the salve soothed the burn.

She watched as he placed two bandages over the spot. "Thank you," she said softly.

His eyes found hers again, and the familiar flutter returned.

Cato shook his head. "You should be more careful."

Wendy gave a small smile. "I guess I'm just lucky that you knew what to do."

Darkness clouded his face in an instant. His whole demeanor changed.

"Yeah, well," he said, and stood.

His gaze seemed to focus anywhere but on her now.

"Maybe we should just start planning first thing tomorrow morning."

Wendy's heart sank a little. She knew it shouldn't have, but it did. There was something about Cato that drew her in, and despite how wrong it was, she felt something for him.

"What about dinner?" she asked, but he was already to the door.

"Thanks," he said. "I'll see you in the morning."

With that he stepped into the night.

Wendy looked down at her bandaged hand and wondered just where things had gone wrong. Beneath the sour exterior and softer center lay a dark piece of Cato. The more she knew of him, the more she wanted to know.

CHAPTER EIGHT

I guess I'm just lucky that you knew what to do.

Cato scrubbed a hand over his face as he stared in the mirror in the bathroom. He'd slept like shit the night before and looked about the same.

Why did Wendy have to say that? Of all the things she could have said, it was the one thing that still haunted him from his time before the Lodge. The wounded or dying hybrids hurt during Horatius Group training, or just as punishment.

People like him. But at least he'd survived.

He sighed loudly. It wasn't fair to be angry with her about something she didn't know. Cato knew this. That didn't change the fact that the differences in their lives were right there staring him in the face.

He glanced at the time on the clock next to his bed. It was early still, but he needed to stop by and eat before heading to the ballroom to start the party planning.

He'd come home right after being with Wendy and raided his fridge. There hadn't been much, but he'd found some bread and cheese. Not the dinner he had been planning, but it was better than going to bed hungry.

Cato shook his head and sighed. He might be uncomfortable, but he still had a job to do. Without wasting any more time, he got dressed and tossed on some shoes before heading outside.

He decided to just walk to the breakfast hall. He needed some time to think.

Chilly air still nipped at him, but he didn't mind much. Even when things were much worse, the cold never seemed to bother the hybrids as much as it did the humans around there.

It wasn't like they weren't affected at all, but just much less so. It made sense. A super-soldier would be less useful if they were too sensitive to different climates. Not every fight was in the tropics.

Still, Cato was eager for the coming warmer weather. It would be good to feel the sunshine on his skin and smell the perfume of spring. The winter had been long, dreary, and filled with threats to his people.

Not to mention better weather would aid their travel to the new place. Even if this party changed the relationship with the military, it was only a matter of time before things changed back.

Some crazy would jump the fence and get shot, or some other reporter would try and whip up outrage against the evil "monsters" of Luna Lodge. They'd never win the war of public opinion, no matter how many parties Jill Hope filmed.

The breakfast hall was crowded when he arrived. People were eating quickly before heading to their jobs. He filled his plate full of food on the line and glanced around the room.

With his main job being a guard, he dealt with quite a few of the men on a regular basis, but there were only a few who he considered close friends.

Cato wouldn't say he was a hard person to know. The hybrids all had a shared past, but he still found it hard to connect to the others.

His gaze caught a pair of hybrids in the distance: Nikon and Alair.

Nikon waved him over to where he and Alair were sitting. The two men were guards like him, and over time, they had come to know each other better than most. Although he hadn't shared everything with them, the two seemed to understand that there was always more on his mind.

Many of the other hybrids were leery of the two men. It

wasn't often that the Horatius Group used children from the same family in their experiments, and certainly they hadn't used a lot of twins.

Although the pair weren't actually identical twins, most people thought they were just because they looked so similar. Anyone who spent much time around them quickly learned that, looks aside, the men were very different.

Cato liked them though. They were easy to be around, and there were always things to talk about, despite the fact that Alair could be a bit quiet at times. It was nice having friends.

It was a concept he still wasn't totally sure about. Having fellow men in a squad was one thing, but that was something different than an actual emotional connection beyond the task or job.

"Haven't seen you in a few days," Nikon said with an easy smile. "But it looks like you've been busy."

Cato frowned. "What's that supposed to mean?"

Nikon gave a quick laugh and ran a hand through his blond hair. "It's all over the news. The interview you did with that reporter and that hot soldier chick."

Cato bristled at his comment. Rage bubbled up in him just hearing another man talk about Wendy.

He took a deep breath. He was supposed to be clearing his head, not letting himself get worked up over petty bull-shit.

"Her name is Wendy," he grumbled. "And we were ambushed. Titus and Colonel Hall set this all up. Now we're stuck setting up a party that everyone in the nation is going to be watching. I can't believe I have to help set this shit up."

Nikon gave another laugh. "Well, whatever the reason, it sounds like a great idea to me."

Cato glanced over to Alair who had remained quiet during all of this. "What do you think?"

Alair looked over to him and gave a small smile. "I'm sure

it will be fun," he said, a little sullener than Cato would have expected. Apparently Cato wasn't the only one having a tough time lately.

Nikon snorted. "Don't mind him, he's just mad that he asked out the wrong girl."

Cato frowned. "And how does that happen exactly?"

"It happens when you're a pussy and aren't clear with the person."

Alair glared at his brother, a growl under his words. "What, because you have all this experience with women? You weren't even there, so what the fuck do you know?"

The smile stayed on Nikon's lips, but Cato could see the serious look in his eyes.

"I know that if it were my Vestal," Nikon said, "I'd make sure I was clear with my intentions."

Alair rolled his eyes and looked back to Cato. "You meeting over the party today?" he asked, clearly wanting to change the subject.

Cato shoveled eggs into his mouth. "After breakfast," he said after chewing for a few more seconds.

"And how's that going so far?" Alair asked.

Cato glanced over at him. He still wasn't quite sure what he should say about Wendy, especially with how close they had come several times to kissing. The idea of holding out on his friends didn't sit right with him, though.

"She's my Vestal." He crammed another big bite into his mouth. It gave him an excuse to not follow up right away.

It was better just to get it out. As soon as they met her, they would know what she was and likely what she was to him.

"What?" the two brothers said in unison.

Cato ignored them and took another bite.

"What are you going to do?" Nikon asked.

Cato shrugged as he finished the food on his plate. "Nothing to do," he said. "We have a party to plan, and it isn't exactly the right time for me to get mixed up with the other side."

Alair frowned. "I'm not so sure there will ever be a right time. If you don't take your chance now, you might never have another."

Cato stood. He knew that Alair was right, but there really was nothing to be done about it. Despite what his heart was telling him, getting mixed up with Wendy was a bad idea. Whatever he felt, she was still a soldier.

"You know you can't fight it," Nikon said, all levity from before gone. "No one can fight it."

"No one has yet." Cato shrugged. "It's not like we have hundreds of bonded here."

Alair and Nikon shared a glance.

Cato nodded to them both. "See you later."

It was Alair who stopped him this time. "Happiness isn't something to try and fight. She's not your enemy."

Cato grunted in reply, grabbed his tray, and turned around. Neither of the other men said anything else as he walked toward the nearest stack of dirty trays.

Sometimes a man had to sacrifice his own happiness to ensure the happiness of others. There was no life with Wendy, especially when they were planning to escape the very people she worked for. The government would probably declare the hybrids fugitive and try and hunt them down.

He and Wendy came from different worlds, and trying to make it into something it could never be was only going to confuse things down the line. All the talk of love wouldn't change any of that.

For now he needed to just keep his head in the game so he could at least be of some use to his people.

CHAPTER NINE

WENDY FULLY EXPECTED the day to be awkward as hell with Cato, especially after the way he had left the night before. The way he bailed so quickly after fixing her burn made a piece of her ache for him.

There was just something in his tone and his face that made her think she'd reminded him of something he'd rather forget. Maybe she was just tricking herself and trying to make it all into something more than it was, but the pain she sensed seemed all too real.

After her arrival at the ballroom, she realized the day would be anything but awkward. Mostly because they didn't have time for awkward exchanges.

The minute Wendy and Cato stepped into the room, a huge number of people greeted them, their crew for the party. Florists, caterer, DJs, waitstaff, a practical event army.

It was a race to keep up with the chatter, questions, and the complaints. Oh, the complaints! Each person had a mountain of complaints about the timeline of the whole event.

It's impossible... especially with this budget.

Can't you just move it back a month?

It's almost a two-hour drive to get here from our building.

We're glad for the business, but our normal policy for an event this large is at least six weeks' notice.

And on, and on, and on.

Wendy swore if she heard one more time about how little notice they had been given, she was going to start taking volunteers for rifle range dummies.

The government and the Lodge were about to throw piles

of cash at them, and yet they still wanted to bitch. She half wondered if some of them were just complaining in an attempt to squeeze out more money from their clients.

She noticed Cato didn't say much as the different people gave their spiels. It wasn't that he was shirking his duties. He was carefully listening and watching each presentation.

Occasionally, he would wrinkled his nose or grunt in agreement, but he seemed to want to leave it to her to make the final decisions.

She wasn't sure if she should be happy he wasn't being unreasonable or annoyed that he didn't seem to have more of an opinion. After all, the whole point of having a hybrid paired with a soldier was that the hybrid could offer his feedback on what the hybrids might like.

He just didn't seem to have any strong preferences. Maybe all the hybrids didn't. The hybrids had lived a spartan lifestyle before freedom, and it wasn't exactly like luxury and fun seemed to be a big part of their current lifestyle either.

It didn't matter. By the end of it all, they had a decent plan for the party. It was going to be an elegant affair, but still relaxed enough that both sides would feel comfortable.

At least she hoped so. Cato didn't seem to have any complaints anyway.

The florist had been irritated they were going with seasonal flowers instead of the red roses he suggested about a million times. Somehow adding roses would have made the whole thing seem like something it wasn't supposed to be. This was a mixing of soldiers and hybrids, not some sort of romantic ball.

The last thing she wanted to do was make it seem like she was setting the mood or something. As it was, she was having a hard time keeping her mind out of that realm. She'd hoped yesterday she'd just been a bit confused, but after a whole day in close contact with Cato, there was no way she could deny her strong, burning attraction to him.

Despite herself, she couldn't seem to take her eyes off Cato throughout the day, no matter what he was doing. Now, she watched him as she arranged the table displays from across the room.

Being the tallest and strongest in the room, he walked from place to place with the main decorator as they decided just where the various decorations would go. Over and over the huge hybrid was forced to hold a red string against the wall.

Seeing the huge man grim-faced as he helped decide where to hang party decorations did add a bit of levity to the situation. Even those actions impressed her.

She knew it must have been driving him crazy, but he still continued on without any complaints other than a few grimaces and grunts here and there.

For her part, though, she needed to concentrate on her own work. She tore her attention away from Cato to attend to continue setting up the example table displays. They'd eventually need to recruit some others for set up, but it wouldn't do any good until they had finished displays to show to people.

"Would you come over for a moment?" someone called to her.

Wendy looked up from the glass rocks she was placing in a vase. Vincent, the decorator, stared down at her.

"I'd just like to get your opinion," he said, a bit of a frown on his face. "Your friend isn't being much help."

Wendy sighed. Cato wasn't being helpful? They stepped over to where Cato stood on the ladder.

Cato glanced between Vincent and her before shrugging. "I told you, I don't know about this shit."

The twitch of his mouth suggested he was reaching his limit.

Vincent sighed dramatically. "This is not... shit." He glared at Cato. "This is the difference between the Van De

Fleur affair and the Montgomery fiasco. I will not be humili-
ated again." He crossed his arms.

Wendy didn't have the slightest idea what the hell either
of those parties were, but it was clear Vincent was having
none of that.

She glanced over to Cato who was staring at the decorator
like he'd sprung a second head.

Of all the things she'd imagined being responsible for
when she received word of the unit's assignment to Luna
Lodge, playing diplomat between a decorator and a hybrid
was probably about last on the list.

"Of course," Wendy said with just the slightest twitch of
her mouth. "We wouldn't want that."

Vincent nodded, glad that someone finally agreed with
him. "If you wouldn't mind doing it again," he said to Cato.

Cato muttered something under his breath.

She couldn't quite catch everything he was saying, but she
was fairly certain that he'd said something about "head" and
"ass." Neither of which, she assumed, were meant in a pleas-
ant way.

Wendy might have snickered if she hadn't looked back up
to Cato and been totally mesmerized by the bare skin that had
been exposed when he lifted his arms up.

The tan skin there pulled tightly over the flexed muscles.
A light dusting of dark brown hair ran a path down the middle and disappeared into his pants.

She swallowed hard. Her mouth suddenly dry. The
thought of running her tongue along the path made her center wet.

Pure white heat radiated from her center, and for a moment she forgot just what she had been doing.

"What do you think?" Vincent asked.

Her gaze trailed up to where Cato stood staring down at
her. His normal amber eyes were glowing now. Wendy
watched as he took in a deep breath and heard a low rumble

come from him.

The sound made her nipples tighten under her shirt. Suddenly she was entirely too sensitive. The bra she wore scraped against the hard peaks, and she had to take in several deep breaths to keep from moaning.

A little skin and she was already more turned on than she'd ever been in her life. Whoa.

"Is nobody going to give an opinion here?" Vincent huffed.

Her attention snapped over to the other man, and she could feel the heat in her cheeks.

"Yeah," she said with as much enthusiasm as she could muster. "That looks good."

Vincent smiled. "It really does," he said. "Okay, that's good for today. I'll just pack up a few things and be on my way."

Wendy nodded. She barely heard what Vincent had been saying. Her body was far more aware of the giant hybrid climbing down the ladder so very close to her.

Cato came to stand next to her, and she could feel the heat from him as he leaned in a little.

Despite that, she couldn't even look him in the eye, she was so embarrassed. Getting caught staring at a guy's package area.

Wendy looked up to the large man in front of her. "I'm so sor—"

His mouth closed the distance between them, and she barely had time to think before his mouth was on hers.

It was insane. They weren't alone. Sure, there wasn't anybody else left at this point but Vincent, but still…

The kiss was hot and forceful, demanding she follow him where he was leading.

She did. Wendy kissed him back with everything she had. The burning inside her only flared hotter when he pressed her against the wall, his knee pressed between her hot thighs.

A small explosion burst in her panties, begging her to just rub a little against his leg.

Suddenly there was cold air between them, as if Cato hadn't just had her wrapped in the hottest kiss she'd ever had.

"I think I've got everything," Vincent called from over at the table.

She turned and saw him smiling at the table, seemingly unaware of what had just taken place.

When Wendy looked back over to Cato, she could see the ragged way he was breathing and the large bulge in his pants.

"I've got to see Titus," he said gruffly.

She watched, unable still to say anything as he stormed out the ballroom door.

Vincent came to stand beside her and sighed a little. "Now that is one hell of a man."

CHAPTER TEN

CATO STORMED PAST AVA'S DESK, throwing open the office door. He stomped into Titus's office.

The leader of Luna Lodge looked up from his computer, quirking a dark eyebrow. "Yes?"

"I can't do this," Cato said.

Ava trailed behind him. A quick glance over his shoulder revealed a deep frown on her now red face.

Titus nodded to her, and Cato watched as she shot him one last dirty look before closing the door.

"You can't do what exactly?" Titus asked. He remained behind his desk, calm and undisturbed by the sudden outburst. If anything, the faint smirk on his face suggested he was amused.

Cato paced back and forth in the office, his heart thumping. He'd not been this worked up outside of battle. He ran a hand through his hair.

He'd kissed Wendy. No excuses. It had been all him, and there was no changing what he'd done.

He shook his head. She just looked so perfect there. Her cheeks still pink from the arousal he'd smelled on her. It had been hard enough waiting until that decorator was looking the other way. If the man weren't there, Cato might have not wanted to stop at kissing.

He could still taste her. The sweet honey taste from her mouth mixed with the rich cinnamon of her arousal intoxicated him. He wasn't sure how he'd lasted so many years without her.

There was no way he'd be able to keep himself from her after this. Given the way she kissed him back, it didn't seem like she was displeased with the idea.

"I can't work with that woman," Cato said, practically shouting.

Titus raised a brow and folded his hands in front of him. "Is there something wrong with her?"

Cato shook his head. "There's nothing wrong with her. There's something wrong with me. I can't concentrate when she's near. How am I supposed to follow the mission when I'm constantly distracted?"

He looked over to Titus who seemed unsurprised by his words. Maybe he expected that he would react like this. After all, she really was the first woman he'd ever worked with before.

"I have faith in you," Titus said. "I'm sure you'll do what needs to be done."

Cato had to let him know the severity of the situation. He'd assumed Titus had already figured things out, but that might have been assuming too much.

"You don't understand. She's my Vestal."

He stopped pacing for a moment and looked down at his shoes. It was embarrassing having to admit that he couldn't control himself because his urges were making him half crazy.

"I know. If anything, I may have known before you."

Cato's head shot up, and he stared directly at Titus who continued to sit comfortably behind the desk. "What?"

Titus sighed and leaned back in his chair. "We assigned you to Wendy because we knew there was compatibility and wanted to test it."

Cato stood stunned. That hadn't been at all what he was expecting. "So you knew that she was my Vestal and set this up?"

Titus sighed. "We suspected," he said. "On a previous mission, we found a list of some Vestals that the Horatius Group knew of. Wendy just happened to be on the list. It was luck that she was here and could be our chance to gain some insight with what the military is planning and if this current unit has any direct connections to the Group."

Cato's pulse thundered in his ears. They had set him up. His own people had set him up for this, and now Titus was acting like it was no big deal.

Cato growled. "So this is how it is? You set me up and just treat me like I'm some sort of fucking science experiment?"

Titus shook his head and stood. "It's not like that."

Cato was done with this shit. Being included in on the plans only to be used like some sort of rat. He glared at his great leader.

He growled. "You're no better than the Group."

Titus's face twitched, but he kept his calm expression. "Wait," Titus said as Cato turned to the door. "You don't understand."

Cato stopped at the door. "I understand just fine." He stormed out.

He could hear Titus calling for him but didn't stop. The pain in his chest wouldn't let him. It was a betrayal. They might not see it that way, but it was. Being moved around just to see how things played out.

So, in the end, it'd be the same. All the freedom didn't matter if it just meant a new group of people pulling the strings.

It burned in him that they didn't trust him enough to tell him the purpose of his job. He wouldn't have been adverse. Sacrifice for the job was something he was willing to do.

He kicked open the door outside and took in several deep breaths. "Cato?"

Shit. This was the last thing he wanted.

He glanced over to where Wendy stood, her face shadowed by the setting sun. Even now he felt the pull to her. Maybe that's what they had been hoping for. That the animal would pull him to her, and things would just happen.

It only made him angrier just thinking about it.

"I can't," he said, more to himself than to her.

He stomped away without looking back.

CHAPTER ELEVEN

WENDY DEBATED if she was doing the right thing. Cato seemed so angry before when she'd caught him outside the office building. She just couldn't seem to get the injured way he looked out of her mind even after going home. Between that and the kiss, it was like Cato had invaded her mind.

She glanced down at her clothes as she made her way to his house. Jeans and a t-shirt. Casual. Odd how something so casual could take her nearly an hour to pick out.

She hoped he liked it, but she really had no clue about the kind of clothes he liked. Maybe he really liked a woman in uniform.

Wendy stabbed at some of the doubt creeping into her mind. He'd given her a passionate kiss in public, even if the only witness wasn't looking their way at the time. At minimum, that proved that he harbored more than a little attraction to her.

Heat spread across her cheeks. This was silly. She couldn't be running around like a little school girl because she had a crush. Just thinking the word made her blush even more.

Wendy stopped outside of his place and spun around on her heel. There was no way she was following through on this. It was a bad idea in every single way.

They still had to work together after all. This wasn't any different than getting into relationship with another NCO in her unit. It was just trouble waiting to explode.

"What are you doing here?"

His deep voice hit her right in the center and slowly she turned around.

Wendy held up the six pack of beer she was carrying.

"You seemed like you were having a bad day, so I thought I'd bring some beer over. A little booze always makes a hard day not seem so bad."

He stared at her from behind the half-opened door. All she could make out was his glowing amber eyes in the darkness. The sight was both eerie and beautiful.

Stupid. She had been so stupid. Maybe the kiss was just some hybrid instinct thing and meant nothing to him. Maybe he was just trying to make some sort of point.

"Come inside."

She stood stunned for a moment as she watched him step inside the house, leaving the door open for her.

Still unsure, Wendy climbed the steps and crossed through the open door.

The inside wasn't much different from her own place. Maybe nicer furniture, but the layout was fairly similar. The only real difference between the two was that he had a fireplace near the couch.

Not really certain what to do, she stepped farther into the room and closed the door. Whether this night would prove a bad idea or not, she'd made the move in response to his kiss.

Cato sat on the couch, not saying anything. He stared ahead at the crackling flames in the fireplace. Wendy sat down on the farthest end of the couch and placed the beer on the table. It was then she noticed the bottle of whisky and empty glass.

Apparently he'd already bought into the idea that a little booze could help the hard day go away.

She wasn't sure what to say. Whatever was troubling him weighed heavy on his mind. This didn't just seem to be about an uncomfortable day of party planning.

"Maybe I should go."

She started to stand when a strong hand came out and held her forearm.

"Stay," he said quietly.

It wasn't a request, but a plea. He needed her. Cato wasn't the sort to say it, but she could just feel it. Not just feel, she knew.

She nodded and sat back down on the couch.

"Would you like some?" he asked, holding up the bottle.

Wendy shrugged. She wasn't afraid of a little hard alcohol. Maybe sharing a drink of the whisky would help open him up.

Cato stepped into the kitchen and came out with a matching glass with a few pieces of ice. He poured some whisky into each glass and handed it to her.

Wendy took a drink. The heat burned down her throat and warmed her stomach instantly.

She watched as he took several large swallows before setting the glass down and looking her way.

"Do you ever feel like you have no control over your life?"

"Every day." She gave a small smile. "I'm in the military. I don't have control over my life."

He nodded, picked his glass up off the table, and leaned back against the couch with a sigh. Cato rested the glass against his leg with his hand and let his head flop back on the top of the cushion.

"I just feel like every piece of my story is written, and I didn't get to have a say in anything." He flexed his fingers on his other hand into a fist and back several times. "From the day I was fucking born."

Cato lifted the glass and finished off the liquor there.

Wendy took several swallows herself before placing her glass on the table. She could already feel the soft effect it was having on her head.

"My childhood, my job, even who I'll love," he said, and sighed. "It's all been decided, and I didn't even get to offer an opinion."

She started to think that over in earnest when her mind

snapped back to a single word: love.

She leaned forward a little, unable to stop herself from being interested. She still understood so little about how the hybrids actually lived their lives.

"Do you have arranged marriages or something?" she said.

Her heart hammered in her chest. More and more she found herself hoping that what she'd felt before wasn't one-sided, and that coming there wasn't some horrible mistake.

Cato rolled his head to the side to look at her. His amber eyes flared up for a moment, and she had to fight to keep her breathing under control.

"Yeah. Something like that," he mumbled.

The kiss started to make sense. He'd probably just found out his marriage was arranged. He didn't have a lot of women around him, and so he kissed the only one he could find, a sort of rebellion against his marriage.

The anger she'd seen earlier must have been from him meeting with Titus and being told he'd have to go forward with the marriage regardless of what he wanted.

She fought a sigh that wanted to come out. That passion had been real. There had to be more than just rebellion to it.

Wendy licked her lips and leaned in a little more. She was playing a dangerous game, but she had to know the truth.

"And what would you choose to do?"

"If I chose the same thing, would it really be me making the decision?" he whispered.

Cato leaned her way slightly. Their bodies were close enough now that his heat wrapped around her. It made her remember the heat from earlier during their kiss. The passion that had flowed between them.

She couldn't think. Her eyes were so focused on his it was hard to think on much of anything.

"If the outcome is the same, does it really matter?" she managed to whisper.

Cato stilled.

Shit. What had she just said? Was she telling him to go in-to his arranged marriage? That hadn't been her intent. He asked a question, and she just answered without thinking.

"Of course, I could be wrong," she sputtered.

A soft smile spread across his face, and she was stunned for a moment. He was handsome, no question, but seeing this side made her heart thump wildly in her chest.

"You're right," he said as he placed his empty glass on the table. "It doesn't matter."

Wendy expected to be told to leave. To be pushed away to make room for this new woman.

What she didn't expect was for him to swoop her into his arms. Her legs straddled his lap while his mouth covered her own in a toe-curling kiss.

She pulled back after a moment to stare down at him in shock. "What about what your leader wants?"

Cato shrugged. "I've made my choice."

CHAPTER TWELVE

CATO KISSED HER HARD. The spicy whisky mingled between their mouths, and he tightened the hold he had around her waist. Wendy relaxed into him, her soft body flush against his own.

His. His Vestal. His other half.

She was his. It didn't matter what some stupid paper said, or what anyone thought. She was his because the idea of her not being with him alone made his heart ache. Made him fear a darkness of eternal loneliness.

He'd show her that she was his. Show her that they couldn't exist apart.

He pulled away from her mouth and placed soft kisses along her neck. His hands slipped under her t-shirt. He groaned when he reached the soft skin there.

Cato made his way back to her mouth now. Their tongues mingled as he ran his hands over her skin. He was already hard, but there were so many things they could do first. He continued to wrestle her tongue.

Wendy surprised him. The kiss they had shared earlier was explosive, and he had wondered if it was a fluke, but if anything, the new kiss was even more so. One of her hands moved behind his head, urging him as she moved her mouth over his. Her other gripped his shirt as if it were the only thing keeping her there.

Not that he was going anywhere. He needed her. It didn't matter that they were taking things fast. He needed to feel her. To taste her. To be inside her. A low rumble escaped his chest.

He pulled his mouth away from her and stared into her

beautiful green eyes. No matter how much he wanted her, she needed to understand before he went too far.

"I can't wait," he said softly. "Tell me now if we should stop."

Wendy shook her head, and he groaned as he pulled her braid out of its confines and watched her soft hair as it framed her face. He kissed her again now with an urgency he hadn't felt before. She was his, and he needed to show her.

Cato stood, and she wrapped her legs around his center. Wendy looked up to him in surprise.

Without a word, he carried her back to his room.

Wendy's head spun as he dropped her onto the bed. It was all going so fast, but there wasn't a part of her that wanted things to stop.

She wanted Cato. No. She needed him. Needed to feel him inside her.

She could already feel the burn between her legs and was desperate to have him alleviate the ache there.

It was dark in his room. Wendy couldn't see his body like she'd hoped, but it didn't stop her hands from moving freely over his body as he discarded their clothes. It seemed like only a few seconds passed before they were rolling naked in the bed. Their bodies pressed against one another as they kissed.

He was a hell of a kisser. Each kiss left her hungry and desperate for more.

When he slid his mouth from hers to trail hot kisses down her neck again, Wendy couldn't stop the loud moan that escaped.

Cato traveled lower and lower, gently sucking on her hard nipples as he did. And still even lower. Down her soft belly until his hot breath was at her opening. The warm air summoning even greater heat.

"I'm not really—" she said.

"I need to taste you." His voice was rough with need.

His tongue slipped between her folds and along her hot clit. She jumped at the feeling of him there. A zing of excitement zipped through her. Another moan escaped.

He lapped at her opening with just enough pressure to her clit to keep her wanting more but never enough to send her over the edge. Her toes curled as the pressure continued to build.

Cato reached up to pinch her nipples. A slow twinge of pain radiated from her nipples as he continued to torture her lower half.

Without warning, he slid his tongue deep inside her. Wendy balled her fists into the mattress as she tried to fight for control. Still, she wanted more. She wanted him, all of him.

He pushed into her again, each time going farther than the last. Wendy ran her hands through his soft wavy hair and gave a little pull.

"Please," she whispered. "I need you."

A low growl came from him. She could feel it as the sound vibrated off her wet center. It only heightened her need for him.

She felt the bed shift around her as he placed his body over hers. Wendy spread her legs wide and sighed when he settled between them.

Cato shifted slightly, and she could feel his length pressed against her.

"Holy shit."

He went perfectly still, and in the darkness she could see his now-glowing amber eyes as they stared down at her.

"Should I…"

His voice trailed off and melted her heart.

Wendy reached up and wound her hand around his neck, pulling Cato in for a soft kiss. She could taste herself on him, and it only turned her on more.

When she pulled back, she smiled at him.

"I was surprised," she said. "That's all."

Cato continued to stare at her. His body was pulled slightly away as if he was still worried about continuing.

Not wanting to wait, Wendy reached between the two of them until her hand wrapped around his hard cock.

She stroked him and let off a string of exclamations inside her head. Large was not the word for something like this. She'd seen large, and this wasn't it.

Massive. Cato was massive when it came to tools.

The more she stroked him the more she really wondered if he would fit. It wasn't like she didn't have any experience, but nothing like this.

Although she figured with as turned on as she was, it wouldn't be as much trouble as she worried. She was slick as a river at this point.

His fingers found her clit and did a few circles. That was all it took for her to be right there at the brink of her orgasm again. She sucked in a deep breath.

Unable to stand much more, Wendy guided his head to her opening.

"Maybe we should—" he said.

Wendy leaned forward until her mouth was at his ear. "Shut up and fuck me," she whispered.

She felt him grow in her hand as he slowly entered her wet center.

Never in his life had he been so turned on. Her tight pussy gripped him as he pressed in farther.

Cato stared down at Wendy. Her mouth open slightly, cheeks pink, and mouth red from his kisses. She thrashed her head back and forth, moaning the deeper he pushed.

"More," she moaned.

Fuck. Every time she did something like that, he had to fight to keep from burying himself to the hilt.

Her hands gripped his hips, and she pulled hard on him unexpectedly.

Cato lost his balance and sank hard into her pussy.

"Yes," she hissed against his ear.

His heart throbbed to his brain. Or maybe that was his dick throbbing. Whatever it was, he was trying not to shoot his load before they had even started.

Her hands held him firmly inside her. Cato could feel her nails biting into his ass, and it only excited him more with how much she wanted him.

"Go slow," she whispered.

He grunted. Speaking was something that he didn't seem to be able to do at the moment. It was taking everything he had to just keep focus on what he was doing.

Slowly he pulled out of her until just the tip of his cock was inside. Then he pressed back into her.

With each movement, her pussy gripped him. It was like sweet torture being inside her.

"More," she moaned.

Cato struggled. He wanted to go faster, but she was so damn tight. Last thing he wanted was to hurt her.

Wendy groaned loudly, and he stopped his movement.

"Lay down," she said.

Cato felt his heart sink. He'd ruined the moment with his lack of experience.

He lay on the bed next to her and tried to think of ways he could make it up. Maybe with time he would get better.

A leg swung over his body, and he nearly roared when Wendy sank down hard over his throbbing erection. She brought her face close to his.

"I won't break," she said as if she had been reading his thoughts.

With that she lifted her body and slammed back down on him hard. His head thrust even deeper inside her.

Cato brought his hands to her hips, desperate to keep the movement up.

With ease he helped her move over him, sliding her wet

pussy over his aching cock over and over.

Her tits bounced with each thrust, and it mesmerized him.

"Faster," she groaned. "I'm so close."

He felt himself grow even more and knew she wasn't the only one.

Cato slipped her over onto her back. This time he had no reservations as he hammered into her.

Wendy moaned and thrashed as his cock slammed into her, their hips slapping with the force of his effort.

On the edge of his orgasm, Cato reached between her legs and rubbed hard against the bundle of nerves there.

She clenched hard around him as her insides became even slicker.

With two hard thrusts, he came inside her. Her wet pussy still pulled on him as he did.

Cato leaned over her, making sure not to rest his full weight on the woman beneath him.

"Amazing," she whispered.

It was just a word, but the way she said it touched the dark parts of him and chased them away.

Cato rolled over and pulled her tightly against him, as if to protect the special thing he'd found.

CHAPTER THIRTEEN

No matter how much Wendy tried, she just couldn't stop smiling. All morning long she had been smiling while she worked on the decorations, so much so that even Vincent commented on it.

"You certainly seem chipper," he said.

"Uh, just got a good night's rest."

A knowing smirk appeared on his face. "Somehow I doubt that."

In truth, she was so happy at that moment, she couldn't work up any embarrassment. Vincent seemed content to not press her on it either.

It didn't help that Cato was always around her, whether it was hanging up something for Vincent or piecing together the dance floor they had ordered. Many times he'd stretched in a way that would show off his delicious muscles, the same ones she'd explored with her hands, legs, and mouth.

He didn't smile like she'd seen the night before, but every so often she would find his eyes on her, and a flush would trickle down her body. It took all her Army discipline not to suggest they sneak out for a mid-afternoon quickie or to run over and lick him.

She really wanted him, and she knew he really wanted her.

Wendy had never felt like this in her life. It wasn't exactly easy to make a woman in the Army feel like a delicate thing to be cherished, but that's exactly how she felt.

"No, no, no, not there," Vincent shouted.

Cato grunted. "Just point."

She bit back a laugh.

* * *

When Wendy headed out to lunch, she'd regained some small ability to not grin like an idiot, but it still slipped through. After grabbing her food from the line, she spotted Leah and Jamie. The pair waved to her, and she headed toward them.

She exhaled and tried to not smile so much. They were like emotional sharks. They'd smell last night on her if she gave them any reason to suspect something had happened, but she wasn't going to avoid her friends just because she'd gotten laid.

"Hello," Wendy said, and took a seat.

"Heya," Jamie said.

Leah nodded and swallowed a spoonful of her soup.

Wendy decided to taste a bit of her sandwich, as the pair continued on a conversation she'd apparently interrupted with her arrival. Besides, she wanted to spend a little more time thinking about her evening fun.

She took a bite of her sandwich, ignoring the idle chit-chat between Jamie and Leah for the moment. She didn't really want to get into anything lengthy anyway, as she wanted to get back to the party preparations sooner than later.

Wendy almost wanted to laugh. She'd been so worried about the assignment, but it was turning into one of the easiest and most enjoyable of her entire time in the Army. Before she knew it, a broad smile appeared on her face.

"Oh my God!" Jamie squealed. "I know what that shit-eating grin means. You got laid!"

Stupid Jamie.

Wendy almost choked on her food. Several of the men around them stopped what they were doing to listen in. Great, now her love life would be gossip fodder for the hybrids and soldiers.

After finishing swallowing her food, Wendy turned to glare at Jamie. "Ever heard of privacy? Maybe you should say it for the guys in the back. Don't think they heard you. Maybe we can get on the PA system and announce it all over Luna Lodge. Or send an e-mail out to everyone in my unit and the Lodge."

Jamie rolled her eyes. "But you don't deny it."

Shit. Wrong move.

"Interesting," Leah said, a faint smirk on her face. "Really interesting." She eyed Wendy for several seconds. "So I take it your party plans are going well."

Wendy tried to play it cool. Maybe she could trick them off the hunt. "They're going fine." She waved a hand. "Everything is nearly done. All we really need to do after today is set things up for Sunday." She shrugged. "Maybe if I ever leave the Army, I could start an event coordination business." She chuckled, hoping her banter would distract them from the events she'd rather not talk about.

"That well, really?" Leah stared at her for a moment. A dangerous grin appeared on her face. "So what I'm hearing you say is that you're free to bring your stud out with us tonight."

Wendy froze. Shit. Wrong move again. It's like they were playing chess, and she was playing checkers.

Her mind reeled as she tried to come up with a half-way decent excuse. "I really don't think—"

She stopped talking when she noticed the two women staring directly behind her. She inhaled deeply, and a familiar scent reached her nose. She turned and found Cato standing there, tray of food in hand.

"I just thought I would…" he said with a shrug.

Leah smiled up at him. "Have a seat. We were just inviting the two of you out tonight. I thought it'd be fun to have another couple."

Cato sat down next to Wendy, and heat spread over her face from his nearness. "Out?" he asked.

Wendy responded first. "It's not really out but to the E-

Club." He nodded and turned his attention to the roast chicken on his plate. She wondered if he'd ever been there before. "They... we're going with Alair and Nikon."

Cato brought up his head from his food and stared between Jamie and Leah, a curious look on his face.

"Friends of yours?" Wendy asked.

Cato nodded. "Yeah." He looked over to her, his bright eyes staring directly into her soul. "So a date?"

She wasn't sure if he was asking her on one, or if they should call it a date. Wendy placed her hand on his thigh. She wasn't quite sure what they had together, but she didn't want it to end with a one-night stand. And Cato was giving every indication that he wanted something more.

"That would be nice." She smiled.

Jamie let out an exaggerated sigh. "I'm getting second-degree burns from the heat you two are giving off."

Cato looked down at his lunch while Wendy glared at her mood-killing friend. She'd have to have a talk with her later.

With just a few bites, Cato managed to eat everything on his plate and stood.

Wendy could see he was at his social limit. Cato wasn't a guy who said much, and despite how angry he might look, inside was a man who cared far more than he let on. Maybe that was why he'd been assigned to help with the party.

Cato looked over to Leah. "What time?"

"We figured we'd all meet at the club at 7:15."

He stared down at Wendy. "I'll pick you up at 7:00."

She nodded. The heat coming back to her cheeks.

She watched as he walked away. Her gaze slid down his back and landed on the firm ass now covered by jeans.

"Yeah, I'd totally stare at that all day," Jamie said.

Wendy turned to stare in shock at her friend.

Jamie shrugged. "What? He's worth the stare."

Wendy took another bite of her sandwich. "I thought you had a date tonight. Shouldn't you not be staring at other men's asses?"

Jamie winked. "Date, not a wedding." She leaned in a little. "But more importantly, what are you going to wear?"

"Jeans and a t-shirt."

Wendy took another bite of her sandwich. The thought hadn't even crossed her mind. It wasn't like it was that big a deal. After all, he'd already seen her with her clothes off. He doubted he was going to judge her over not being fashionable.

Jamie dropped her fork on her plate.

Leah chuckled. "To be fair, it's an improvement from her yoga pants."

Wendy glared at Leah. "Thanks," she said sarcastically.

"There is no way you're going on a date with that sexy hunk of man meat dressed like a hobo," Jamie said with force.

Wendy scoffed. "Hobo? Really?"

Jamie ignored the protest. "Either you pick something, or I will."

Wendy winced. There was no way in hell she was letting Jamie pick her clothes. Most exposed a bit too much for her taste, and the last time she'd done so, she spent most of the night trying to either pull the material up or down depending on what area decided to show off too much.

"Fine," she said, and took a large bite. "I'll wear the black dress."

Jamie looked like she wanted to protest but stopped because of the death stare Wendy was giving her.

"Great," Leah said. "Looks like a fun night of date, date, and pretend date."

Wendy felt bad for her friend. Despite her homebody-like ways, she knew Leah wanted to find someone. Unfortunately, it might be that Luna Lodge just wouldn't be the place for that.

"You never know, Nikon might be the one," Jamie said.

Leah rolled her eyes. "Don't think I'll hold my breath on that one."

Wendy glanced over to Jamie. They grew quiet for a moment, their mutual worry for their friend evident.

Leah sighed. "Hey," she said after a moment. "I'm fine. Really." She smiled at them both. "I'm just glad to spend some time with my girls."

Wendy smiled back. She'd missed this. A good set of female friends she could count on that cared, but who weren't plugged into the Army.

"Yeah," she said. "I'm glad to have you both." They both turned to look at her. The one least prone to getting mushy had just gone there. "What? Stop looking at me, or I'll take it back."

They broke out into laughter, and all the tension from before eased away. The night was going to be great. She'd make sure.

CHAPTER FOURTEEN

WENDY'S HEART THUMPED. Maybe she was a mess. Maybe she wasn't hot. She wasn't quite sure.

She'd made sure to wear the tight black dress that showed just a little too much cleavage for a woman who prided herself on her military professionalism, not to mention the matching black bra and panties. But she wanted Cato to see her in more than yoga pants, jeans, or a uniform.

Wendy smoothed over her dress one more time as she stared in the mirror. Her hair was down, and instead of the crimped look she usually got from having her hair in a braid all day, soft blond locks flowed down over her shoulders. Everything looked good to her, but the question was what Cato would think.

A knock came at the door, and she sucked in a breath and let it out slowly. It was go time.

When she opened the door, Wendy was surprised to find Cato in something other than a t-shirt. Tonight he wore an untucked casual light blue shirt along with a pair of dark blue jeans. The shirt fit tightly across his chest, and she couldn't help but fixate on the wide expanse.

"You look amazing," he said quietly.

Wendy sought out his eyes and blushed when they brightened a tad. Something about his glowing eyes enticed her. Or maybe it was just his body in that shirt and jeans.

"You too," she said, her voice coming out with a breathy quality.

Tonight was different. This wasn't getting caught up in a moment of passion, but a genuine, honest-to-goodness date. That meant this was turning from a one-night stand into the beginning of a relationship.

They stepped outside together, and he led her to the car. She gave a small smile as he opened the door for her and then made his way to the other side.

Great in bed and a gentleman. She couldn't remember the last time someone held the door open for her.

In silence, they made their way to the enlisted bar. It wasn't far away, so it wasn't an awkward silence but instead a sort of shared silence where neither of them felt strange about not talking.

Comforting, really. She'd not known him all that long, but it felt like she'd known him all her life, like he understood her on a level that no man had ever understood her.

Wendy almost shook her head. She was already so wrapped up in Cato. Maybe she was pulling a Jamie and letting her heart get carried away. Still, she couldn't deny what she felt.

When they arrived, she took the hand he offered to help her out of the car, but stopped them from walking any farther.

"We don't have to stay long," she said. "I love them, but I also know my friends can be a little much."

Cato leaned in and placed his mouth next to her ear. "If we leave early it's not going to be because of your friends," he said quietly. "It's going to be because looking at you in that dress is pure torture, and I need to be inside you."

A hot blush swept across her face and down her neck. Her center warmed more than a little. Wendy didn't think she'd ever been talked to like that, and she found it turned her on like she'd never been before.

His thick hand slipped into hers as they made their way into the bar.

* * *

The music thumped, shaking the floor and the walls. This was one of the few times Cato wished he didn't have enhanced hearing.

He didn't really care much for the sound, but did accept it was part of the bar atmosphere. Besides, he'd put up with just about anything right now after seeing Wendy in a dress like that. Plus, if he wanted to be with her, he'd need to earn the respect of her friends. At least he knew they already liked hybrids.

Cato wrapped his arm protectively around her waist as they made their way inside. More than a few men looked their way.

Good. He wanted them to see her with him. He wanted them to understand that she was his.

They found her friends sitting with Alair and Nikon at the back of the room. He could already tell that things were going all right for Alair. The quiet one was sitting next to his brother while Nikon was sitting beside the more enthusiastic date. He might still have a chance to salvage the night and end with the woman he actually wanted.

"I see you let the big dogs out to breathe," Jamie said.

Wendy glared at the woman next to Alair. "Jamie, you have no fucking tact." She blushed.

Cato nodded to Alair and Nikon. The other two hybrids shared a glance then looked at him, surprise clearly written on their faces.

"Thought you weren't the bar type," Nikon said, and winked at him.

Cato grunted. The brothers shared a knowing grin. They knew the deal, and they knew why he was fucking there.

"This is Alair and his brother Nikon," Cato said to Wendy.

She smiled at them both. "I'd heard there were a couple hybrids that were related. Isn't that unusual?"

Nikon nodded.

None of them talked about their past much or the women they came from. It wasn't exactly the best thought to think that the woman who gave birth to you cared so little that she would allow such terrible things to be done and then abandon her child like they were nothing for a little money.

Not only that, they'd left them alone in the clutches of terrible people who could and did whatever they wanted without the slightest restraints of ethics or morality.

Cato shook himself of the dark thoughts. The past was the past. It didn't have to determine the future, and right now he wanted to enjoy his time with Wendy.

The waitress brought over two mugs and another pitcher.

He half-filled his glass, and when Wendy shot him a quizzical stare, he leaned down to whisper in her ear.

"I want to have a clear head for all the things I'm going to do to you."

Nikon choked on his beer and looked away, which did little to hide his stupid grin.

Damn super hearing.

Cato draped his arm over the back of her chair and enjoyed the feel of her small warm body pressed into his and the soft skin at her shoulder.

Jamie placed her beer on the table and smiled. "I'll be right back," she said to Alair. "I just need to powder my nose."

The men watched as she walked away. Cato looked directly at Alair. If he was going to make his move, now was the time.

"Would you like to dance?" Alair said to Leah.

The quiet woman stared at him in shock. "But you asked Jamie out."

Alair shook his head and sighed. "I was actually asking you out. It just... things got confused."

Movement caught Cato's attention out of the corner of his eye. He glanced over and saw Jamie standing and staring wide-eyed at Alair.

"I, um, just came back to get my purse," she said. She snatched her purse from the table and ran toward the bathroom.

"Jamie, wait!" Leah shouted over the music.

Cato wasn't surprised at all when Wendy turned to him.

"I've got to go," she said softly.

He nodded.

Wendy raced after her friends to the bathroom. Inside Leah stood beside Jamie.

"I'm so sorry," Leah said.

Jamie shook her head. Her face was red, but she wasn't crying despite how watery her eyes were. "It's my fault," she said. "I was so excited I didn't even think that he might not be talking to me."

"Maybe we should just go home," Leah said.

Jamie shook her head. "No, you can't. I heard a few of the hybrid wives talking about how all this stuff works for them. I don't think I was supposed to overhear because they shut up when they realized I could hear them."

"I don't understand."

"It's not the same as it is for us."

Wendy frowned. "Are you talking about arranged marriages? Cato was saying something, and I think he was talking about that."

Jamie looked at her reflection in the mirror and shook her head. "Arranged marriages? If anything, it's the opposite. Once a hybrid falls for a girl, that's it. It's like fate or something."

Fate. It wasn't a word she associated with love.

The more she thought on it though, the more she wondered. Cato had been so cryptic yesterday during the arranged marriage conversation. Maybe he was trying to break his fate by being with her. Maybe she was the other woman.

Her heart was troubled by it all. She had been thinking it was rushed, and maybe in the end it had been. Maybe he was trying to make something happen that couldn't ever happen no matter how hard he tried. Although from her end, it had been totally real.

She thought about it. The hybrids had been exposed to the world for a while now. A lot of people didn't like them, but it was a big country, and if they could have any wife, it'd make sense that a lot more of them would have been married by now. The fact that there were so few women at Luna Lodge supported what Jamie was saying.

"Go," Jamie said. "Talk with him if anything." She shrugged. "Can't fight fate, right?"

Leah and Wendy stared at the woman in front of them. She wasn't her normal perky self, but she still was the best friend a woman could ask for.

Wendy half expected Leah to refuse, but maybe she felt the pull to the hybrid as well.

"Well," Jamie said and stretched a little. "Can't let all this work go to waste. I'm hitting the floor."

She winked at the two of them. "Wonder if I can get a sandwich dance. Plenty of normal non-fate bound guys around."

Wendy smiled. It didn't take much for Jamie to bounce back, and she was glad. Right now, she had her own troubles brewing.

They left the bathroom and headed back to the table. There was only one thing on her mind at the moment.

"I'd like to go," she said to Cato. "We need to talk."

CHAPTER FIFTEEN

SILENCE SMOTHERED THE CAR RIDE BACK. Cato wasn't sure exactly what had taken place in that women's bathroom, but whatever it was, it didn't look very good for him.

When they stopped outside her place, Wendy didn't wait for him to open the door for her but instead stomped her way to the house. Once at the door, she stopped in the frame.

Cato stepped out to head after her. Maybe Wendy was pissed about his friend upsetting her friend. He could understand that.

"Just what the hell kind of crap are you trying to pull?" she said from the door.

Cato stopped where he was, just a few feet from her, and stared at the very angry woman in front of him. "I don't understand."

She crossed her arms over her chest, pushing up her breasts in such a way that distracted him more than anything.

"I'm not going to be the other woman," she snapped. "I don't know just who you are trying to run from, but if there is some fated women you're supposed to be with, don't go dragging me into your drama." She shook her head. "It's not damn fair!"

Cato stared at her for a moment, not totally sure he was following the conversation. "Other woman?"

She jabbed him hard in the chest with her finger.

"Don't play stupid with me. Jamie told me about your whole fated thing," she said with a bitter laugh. "She overheard some of the wives of the hybrids talking about it. It all makes sense now. All the stuff about making choices."

Her whole body shook as she spoke, her anger and pain

clear to him.

"I'm don't want to be played with," she said and made her way inside. "Good-bye, Cato."

Faster than either of them expected, Cato had her in his arms, unwilling to let her just close the door on his heart like that.

"I don't know what you were told, but there is no other woman. It's always been you. The fates made the choice that my heart already knew was right, and they led me to you."

Wendy stood with her mouth open for a moment, her gaze still pinned on his.

"Now I'm confused," she whispered.

Cato nodded. "Then let me explain."

Wendy stepped out of his arms, and for a moment, he worried she might shut the door on him again. She stepped inside.

"Let's talk," she said.

Wendy watched as Cato closed the door and made his way inside. They sat on the couch, her emotions still on high, and she was not quite sure what the hell was going on. Everything had made sense at the bar, but suddenly she was a jumble all over again.

"The term we use is Vestal," he said. "It's like a purified woman sent from the gods. One half of the heart of a hybrid. Or at least that's how it's told," he mumbled.

"So this is an old wives tale? Some religious myth?"

Cato looked over to her and shook his head. "We used to think so, but more and more we know it to be true. The Vestal is a woman. Her scent is made to draw the hybrid. The two pull each other in with their pheromones. But it's even more than that."

Wendy blinked a few times. More?

"There is one Vestal for a hybrid. One chance at happiness. Once they have bonded, there is no going back for the hybrid."

Wendy kicked off her heels and tucked them under her legs on the couch.

"And how does the bonding happen? Is it like a marriage?"

He shrugged. "Sort of. It's like a bonding of the souls."

She noticed he'd aptly avoided her other question. "How?" she said bluntly.

"You are my bonded," he said. "My heart, body, and soul are already yours."

She opened her mouth and closed it. This was far heavier than she anticipated. Somehow, she had tied herself to Cato. What's more, she wasn't tossing him out the door.

Wendy had never really thought of herself as the marrying sort. Maybe a long-term boyfriend, but marriage? Yet when he talked about being bonded, the very idea of it just seemed right. Not just seemed, felt right, in her heart, maybe even in her soul.

"You don't have to love me," Cato said when she hadn't spoken for some time. "I'm content to just be by your side, but you need to know my feelings. I should have been honest last night before we did anything."

She looked over at him. His face was far more uncertain than she'd ever seen him.

Cato was worried.

Her heart ached at the sight of it, and before she even knew what she was doing, Wendy was moving. She straddled his lap and kissed him on the lips.

It wasn't the searing sort they had shared the night before. This one contained something even more. A feeling. Something more than the words she couldn't seem to find.

When she pulled away, Wendy stared into his soft amber eyes.

"I'm content to be by your side as well," she whispered.

This time she kissed him again. With a bit more passion

than what had been there before, an aching need that never seemed to leave when he was around.

Slowly she undid the buttons to his shirt but stopped when his hands clasped over her own. When she leaned back, she could see the fear there in his eyes.

"Maybe we should go to the bedroom," he said.

Wendy frowned. "I want to see you."

Cato looked away from her and nodded.

She leaned back on his lap as she popped each of the buttons. When she was finished, she pulled the soft cotton away and gasped.

Cato wanted her hands on him. To feel her against him. To think he wasn't some freak, but that's exactly what he was.

He pulled his arms out of his shirt and placed it on the couch next to him.

Wendy placed her small hands on his chest. His muscles tightened under her touch. With slow deliberation, she ran her fingers over the puckered spots that dotted his chest. The scars that were the physical manifestation of his pain.

"Burns," she said softly.

Cato hated them. A sign of his weakness. It was always there, reminding him of just how easily a person's rights could be taken away.

"I was just a teen then," he said. "One of the Horatius Group guards wanted to teach me a lesson after I tried to run on him."

"He burned you like this?"

Cato turned his face away from her. He didn't want her to see this side of him. The one that still felt the pain from it all.

"They held me down as he burned me over and over again."

Cato could still feel the sizzle of his skin and smell the god-awful stench that filled the air.

He jumped when soft lips kissed a sensitive scar on his

chest. Wendy placed a kiss on each one of the spots. When she was finished, she stared back up at him again.

"I don't want you to hide anything about yourself from me," she said softly. "I want to see all of you. Good, bad, and ugly."

His heart filled with a joy he'd never felt before but even more than that, hope.

Cato leaned in and kissed her. His tongue pressed deeply inside, as if he wanted to devour all of her.

With deft hands he slid the black dress over her and onto the couch.

His eyes roved over the black lace that covered her body. He loved every little inch of her.

Soft hands pressed against his pants, and with far more ease than he expected, Wendy unbuttoned and unzipped them. She shoved the material down enough that his cock sprang free of its fabric prison.

"I need you," she whispered to him.

Cato understood. He felt the urgency to be connected to her once again. To fill her up inside as they each reached out for their release together.

He reached down and tore the black panties from her. A small yelp followed.

"I have to be in you," he mumbled.

His fingers brushed across her wet pussy, and he moaned in surprise. She was ready for him.

As if understanding his needs without thought, Wendy lowered herself onto his throbbing cock, taking him in all the way until they were so close that he could no longer see where they were joined.

"So big," she said with a grunt.

Cato stared at her with concern. Despite the beads of sweat that were breaking out on his brow from just the feel of her tight confines, he wanted them both to enjoy it.

He leaned forward and kissed her lightly on the lips.

"Don't push yourself," he whispered.

He groaned loudly near her face when she rose up slightly and then pressed herself back down on him again.

Wendy leaned forward and wrapped her arms around his neck, pressing her mouth against the shell of his ear.

"I'm so turned on seeing your face as I push you deep inside," she whispered. She moaned still near his ear. "When you twitch like that, I can feel it pushing at my cervix," she panted. "It makes my inside shiver."

Damn. She was going to kill him with this sort of talk. But he could feel how deep he was, and the way she flexed around him only added to the pleasure of it all.

She inched up and down him, each time pressing him as far as she could.

Cato gripped her hips hard when she sat down on him again and gyrated her hips, his cock moving inside her as she did.

"Fuck," he said and grunted. "I'm going to come if you keep that up."

Wendy shivered hard in his arms, and she tightened around him, her orgasm shaking her. His cock was still buried deep inside. Every part of her sweet pussy was moving over him, squeezing him in a way he'd never felt before.

Unable to stop, he released inside her. His seed poured against her cervix as it suctioned the tip of his cock.

She collapsed against him. She still shivered as the waves of pleasure wracked her body.

He had never been so drained in his life, but it was all in the best sort of way.

Wendy placed small kisses against his neck, and he could feel the smile there. "You owe me a pair of panties."

Cato laughed. Her comment was totally unexpected.

"Worth it," he whispered.

CHAPTER SIXTEEN

Wendy slipped out of the house early Sunday morning, Cato still sleeping in her bed. They spent the rest of Friday night, along with all of Saturday further exploring both their pleasure and their love.

She ached and was tired, but it was worth it.

That said, duty called. Friday afternoon had been very productive, but they weren't done. The colonel loaned her more than a few lower enlisted, and Titus more than a few hybrids, to help with last minute preparations. Vincent and the other vendors didn't seem to mind the military-grade help.

Despite the fact that everything was nearly ready, Wendy still worried that they had slacked by not at least checking in on the ballroom Saturday. Something might have fallen, or some fool private might have screwed something up.

She decided to walk to the ballroom. It gave her more time to consider her new relationship. Relationship didn't almost seem strong enough to describe something that might have been the result of fate.

Wendy wasn't sure she bought into all of the Vestal story, but she couldn't deny that she'd been drawn to Cato in a way she'd never before experienced. It just felt true.

She let out a quiet chuckle. Lying in bed all day on her day off had been amazing. Thinking on it, she didn't think she'd had a day like that pretty much ever in her life.

Most of her relationships had been when she was just a teen, and when she entered the military, they'd become downright rare. She didn't have the time, and she worried about unit cohesion, so avoided dating the available military men.

Wendy reached the ballroom and stepped in. Surprisingly, Colonel Hall stood inside, her arms folded behind her back.

"Seems like everything is nearly ready," the colonel said.

"Ma'am," Wendy said, and smiled. "I think we were able to pull it off. Still going to be a full day of setting things up and getting the catering in order, but we're ready for this, especially with the added help."

She watched as the colonel walked around the room, examining all the progress they had made. "It seems that you and this man make a good team."

Wendy nodded. "He worked very hard to help make it an affair that all the men will feel welcome at."

Colonel Hall shook her head. "I've also heard that you might be teaming up in a more social way."

Wendy was shocked. Never in the several years she'd been with Colonel Hall had her superior asked her about her private life.

"Ma'am, I didn't think there was any order prohibiting—"

The colonel held up her hand. "Relax, there's no order." She furrowed her brow. "I thought about it, given our position here, but I also realized if I issued an order like that, Titus and his people would take it as a grave insult. It'd make things worse. Plus, I didn't really think it'd be an issue."

"I don't understand, then."

"This isn't about the mission. This is about you as a woman." Colonel Hall sighed. "Take this as friendly advice. This won't end well."

"Why?" Wendy frowned slightly. "Is it because he's hybrid?"

Colonel Hall let out a short laugh.

"Not even the slightest," she said with a smile. "I might be getting up there, but I'm not blind. I get the attraction. They are… the ultimate soldiers."

She winked at her, and Wendy's mouth fell open. This was as frank as she'd ever seen her superior.

"Look, it's not because he's a hybrid. If only it was so simple. It's because he's a man." She patted Wendy on the shoulder. "I've seen you fight your way to where you are. The men respect, you and you work damn hard. You could really go places. I'd just hate to see you throw it all away on some man. Sure, he's an impressive specimen, but he's still a man."

"How is being with Cato throwing things away?"

"You can't be with him. You think you're going to be permanently assigned to Luna Lodge? We might be here years, or they might reassign us in six months. Needs of the Army. Then, what? You going to leave, throw away your career and live with him?" She let out another long sigh. "This is where him being a hybrid matters. The fact that we're here shows how unstable things are. For all we know, next week, everyone will stop caring about hybrids, or maybe they'll kick them all out of the country. Are you ready to sacrifice your entire career for that kind of uncertainty?"

Wendy felt her throat close up. She had worked hard, and she was proud of the work that she had done. All this time she had told herself that a relationship was the last thing she needed. There were goals to be met, and it wouldn't happen with a man in the picture.

Then she met Cato, and he changed everything.

But had he? She still wanted the same things she wanted before. Only now she wanted him there with her. She wasn't even sure that was something she could consider. The fact was that he was a hybrid, and she was still a member of the military.

The colonel was right. Their lives were not their own to direct.

"Just think it over," Colonel Hall said with a sad smile.

Wendy nodded. "Thank you, ma'am. I will."

Her mentor stepped out of the room. Wendy could already feel her heart closing off from the outside world, trying to make a wall so she wouldn't be hurt when she really had to say good-bye to the only man she'd ever loved, maybe the only she ever would.

* * *

Cato hadn't managed to meet up with Wendy before the party started Sunday evening. He'd tried to catch her alone, but it never seemed to work out in his favor. Either someone stepped in the way, or she would slip out without him ever even seeing.

At first, he'd just thought it was the busyness that came with the party. With hundreds of guests and dozens of support staff, it was the largest concentration of people he'd ever dealt with outside one of the protests. In such a situation, it initially made sense that he might not be able to get even a minute of alone time with Wendy.

But he wasn't an idiot. A few times might have been an accident, but it was more than clear that she was doing her damnedest not to be around him. He was starting to think she missed her calling as a super-secret spy.

Even the pesky reporter Jill Hope hadn't been able to catch her for another interview before the big party. Instead Wendy had forced him to do it solo, which didn't go nearly as well. Congenial was something he was not.

That surprised him. She seemed to take her duty seriously, and PR was part of her current task, which meant there was something strong enough to make her risk not doing her best job.

There was no two ways about it, Wendy was avoiding him.

Cato wracked his brain all day with why that would be the case. The last couple days had been amazing, he thought. They'd made love so many times. Each time he'd made sure she was just as satisfied as him.

So much so that he'd made a game of it. How many times he could get her off before he couldn't hold back anymore.

Four times was as high as he'd gotten, but that was mainly because he was so desperate to be inside her he just couldn't hold out.

Cato tugged at the collar of the button-down shirt he was wearing and gave up trying to be as formal as he wanted. He flicked the button and found he could breathe a little better. He still hated the little buttons and slacks he was wearing, but he had wanted to show her that he could look good as well. Or something like that.

Light music played in the background. He glanced around the room. People chatted with one another. Hybrid and human. The event seemed to meet all their expectations, just as he and Wendy had hoped. He could see the cameraman making his way through the party, catching nice shots of people as they seemed to be enjoying things.

"You did well," Titus said as he stepped over to him.

Cato was still pissed at his leader, but he'd take the compliment.

"It was all Wendy," he said stiffly.

Titus laughed. "I somehow doubt that."

Cato turned to frown at him.

"Trouble with the newlyweds?"

Cato grunted. Last thing he wanted to do was talk about his troubles with Titus.

His leader clapped him on the shoulder. "I'm sure it's just jitters," he said. "She'll come around."

He stopped abruptly when Jill made her way quickly in their direction.

"No more interviews," Cato said quickly.

Jill shook her head, and for the first time he could see that the color had washed from her face.

"Where are the children?" she asked quickly.

Cato frowned, but it was Titus who spoke first.

"At home," he said. "What's wrong?"

She shook her head. The normally well put together

woman was shaking and pale.

"I don't know," she said quickly. "It might be nothing, but we just received a tip."

Cato narrowed his eyes. "What sort of tip?"

Jill looked to him, her eyes brimmed in fear. "They said there's a bomb in the building."

CHAPTER SEVENTEEN

WENDY WASN'T JEALOUS. It didn't bother her at all that Cato had been talking to the pretty reporter or that they had stepped out into the hall to continue their discussion.

Jill Hope probably had questions about the hybrid angle. Soldiers weren't exactly rare; hybrids were. There was nothing more to it.

Plus, of course Cato would be talking to Jill and not her. Wendy had spent the entire day doing her best to avoid talking to him, or even being close to him. It wasn't like she could expect him to sit in a corner crying and waiting for her.

Nope. There was no way in hell she was jealous. If only she could convince the pain in her heart that was the case.

Wendy let out a long sigh. She couldn't complain that she'd made a choice and now had to deal with the consequences. After the colonel's little talk, she'd made the conscious decision to distance herself from Cato, at least for a while. If anything to help sort out what the hell she actually wanted.

Why did things have to be so complicated? All she wanted to do was keep the career and the man she had wished for. It seemed unfair that because she was a woman she would have to give up one or the other.

She wasn't even sure if that was the case, even if she wanted to advance higher. It wasn't exactly like married senior female NCOs were unfindable unicorns.

Sure, it could be harder for women, but that didn't make it impossible. Maybe the colonel had to make that choice because of her particular career situation, but that didn't mean the same thing would apply to Wendy.

As a waiter brushed past her, Wendy realized that Colonel Hall wasn't wrong. Cato wasn't just some man, after all. He was a hybrid.

She couldn't ask him to turn his back on his people if she was assigned elsewhere, and that was assuming things didn't get messier for whatever reason.

No matter the problem, she couldn't get Cato out of her head. They were a part of one another. What he had said about souls made sense because she was certain he held a piece of hers.

This wasn't as simple as just passing on a nice boyfriend. The wrong choice might haunt her for the rest of her life.

"Wendy."

The sound of his voice brought her back to just where she was, a busy party.

"I need to talk to you," Cato said.

She turned to glare at him.

He looked so good in his button-down shirt with just a hint of that magnificent chest peeking through. It was no wonder that the reporter had been attracted to him. She was half surprised all the women in the room weren't hitting on him.

The thought soured her mood even more.

"Maybe you should just go talk with your reporter friend again," Wendy snipped.

It was childish and petty and totally not something she meant to say, but the words came out nonetheless.

He moved in quickly. She could smell the aftershave he'd used, and it made her want to move in closer for a better smell. Cato gripped her upper arm in a firm hold.

A grim expression covered his face. "We can talk later about Jill, but right now, we've got a serious problem."

All her jealousy drained away. This wasn't something minor. In the time they had spent with one another, not once had she seen him look so worried.

Wendy scanned the room. She'd been so wrapped up in her pity that she hadn't noticed. A lot of the conversations had quieted. Every hybrid she saw looked worried.

"What's going on?"

Cato shook his head as a waitress passed by with a silver tray full of hors d'oeuvres. "We need to find Colonel Hall. Now."

Wendy nodded. She didn't know what was going on, but she trusted Cato.

They both looked around the room and found the colonel talking with several people.

"Don't raise an alarm," Cato whispered in her ear. "Get her to follow you in the hall. I'll be there with Titus. He can explain."

Wendy nodded and watched as he made his way to the door.

She could do this. The only really issue was how her commander would feel being deceived. There wasn't time to think on that. She either acted on trust or not.

Wendy made her way over to Colonel Hall.

"Sorry to interrupt, ma'am," she said with a bright smile. "I was hoping I might get your opinion on something."

Colonel Hall stared at her for a moment and then turned to the men. "If you'll excuse me for a moment." The took several steps away before Colonel Hall spoke. "What's wrong?"

Wendy looked over to her, surprised that she could even guess.

"Don't be so surprised," the other woman said. "You don't spent years commanding troops and not pick up a thing or two about reading people."

Wendy shook her head as they made their way to the hall. "I'm not sure, but Titus is waiting in the hall."

Colonel Hall nodded. "Understood."

They stepped through the door, and both were surprised

to find about a dozen hybrids standing there.

"What's the meaning of all this?" Colonel Hall snapped, a frown appearing on her face.

"I'm sorry, Maria," Titus said. "We were just informed that there is a possibility that a bomb has been planted in this building."

Wendy looked over to where Cato stood next to the reporter. He nodded for Jill to speak.

"I got a tip that there was a bomb," Jill said.

Colonel Hall narrowed her eyes on the woman. "From who?"

Jill stood a little taller. "I'm not at liberty to say. But I know this is coming from inside the government."

"Our government? The tip?"

"You don't understand." Jill shook her head slowly. "No. The bombing."

Colonel Hall snorted. "That makes no sense. Why the hell would our government want to bomb their own people?"

Titus raised a brow. "Why indeed?" He stared at Colonel Hall. "You're a soldier, you already have to know the truth. Sometimes all it's takes is one ambitious politician, maybe a senator with a grudge, for example, and soon innocent people are getting hurt, and that's not even when a hybrid might be involved."

"You expect me to believe that someone in the US government is coordinating a terrorist bombing on US soil that might get US Army soldiers killed?"

"I expect you to believe that if someone believed the hybrids are a serious enough threat, that a little collateral damage would be considered acceptable losses if they could take us out."

The colonel's face tightened.

Wendy watched as the colonel processed everything she had just heard. She could tell that the whole thing bothered her, but she wasn't going to let that affect how she dealt with the situation.

"If we disrupt this party, and say there's a bomb, the facility will never recover," Colonel Hall said. "If what you say is true, then whoever is pulling the strings will use it as an excuse to try and put more pressure on this place not less." Titus started to say something but stopped when she held up her hand. "We need to assess if there is actually a threat."

Titus nodded. "I'm on it. My men can move silently and smell if there is anything off."

Wendy thought for a moment that the colonel might protest.

"Then we'll rely on your skills," she said. "I'll quietly send a few men to guard the children."

Titus nodded. "Thank you."

Colonel Hall turned to head back inside but stopped just outside the door. "When this is all over, I think you and I should have a talk."

Titus nodded. "Agreed."

She nodded again and walked toward the door. "I need your help, Sergeant."

Wendy chanced a look at Cato. His eyes were following her as she made her way to the door.

"I'll find you," he said.

His words were low, but she still heard them as clear as if he were standing next to her.

She nodded. Her heart beat painfully in her chest as she stepped through the doors.

Danger and uncertainty came with being a soldier. She knew this. They all had a job to do, and they would just have to trust that they would see one another at the end.

CHAPTER EIGHTEEN

TITUS ASSIGNED CATO, ALAIR, AND NIKON to check the back of the building. It was one of the most likely areas for an entry point, as it wasn't as well-lit and the easiest spot to slip in an attacker or bomb.

Clouds covered the sky, leaving dark shadows in the area. The hybrids' superior night vision prevented the night from being too much of a handicap, but it didn't push away the eerie feeling settling over Cato.

It still wasn't clear how the bomb would have gotten in. Getting into the building was one thing and easy, but getting into the Lodge was another.

Ever since the hybrids were made aware of the tunnels running under the Lodge, Titus had made sure they were watched at all times. Lucan was outside the fence, and it was easiest for him seeing as the military still wasn't aware of his presence.

If one of the townspeople had managed to enter the tunnels with a bomb, he should have been able to tell, given his superior smell and the unusual scents involved. But Titus and Sol hadn't received any report from Lucan about unusual traffic in the tunnels. He was checking again, but no one held much hope he'd found anything.

There was always the risk the terrorists were using a spray the hybrids had seen encountered before when dealing with the Horatius group. It prevented hybrids from picking up on normal scent trails. Even then, it left an odd scent that most of them were now familiar with.

The military was watching the fence. It'd make sense if a traitor let in a bomber to kill hybrids, but he doubted they'd be willing to let someone in who might kill hundreds of humans.

Whatever had happened, it wasn't good. Someone would have to pay for a bomb killing human soldiers. The country would want revenge, and scum like the hybrid-hating Senator Woods would be able to deflect the blame from the government or the Group and on to the hybrids.

No matter what, the hybrids would be blamed for this and would likely end up being locked away for good. It would be easy after the hatred they had endured these past few months.

Cato grunted. He still couldn't believe whoever was targeting the party was willing to sacrifice so many humans, but like Titus had told the colonel, they probably considered it an acceptable loss.

Fucking bastards. They acted like hybrids were the monsters, but hybrids would never casually kill their own kind just to take out some of the enemy.

The whole fucking thing just pissed him off. He was sick and fucking tired of people playing with their lives like god, especially such ruthless pricks.

"Nothing over here," Alair said.

Cato nodded. They had swept the area several times but hadn't found anything. They were running out of time.

Something moved in the distance. He clenched his fist and looked that way. If needed, he'd take down a bomber rather than let them get near the building, even if it cost him his own life.

He took in a deep breath and relaxed as the familiar scent of a fellow hybrid reached him. The distant dark shape closed until he could clearly see Lucan.

Lucan sprinted toward him, almost charging, before stopping just a few feet in front of him. He was likely the fastest runner they had at the Lodge.

"Anything at the tunnels?" Cato asked.

Lucan shook his head. "Titus just came by with some of

the other men. Things are quiet tonight at the mill. Entirely too quiet. I made my way inside the gate to just check on things. I don't trust them. Quiet always means trouble."

Cato scrubbed a hand over his face. There was something they were missing. If the townspeople weren't at the mill and weren't in the tunnels, then where in the hell were they?

"Son of a bitch," he muttered.

He turned to the men to explain but stopped when a loud explosion rocked the building around them. It tossed them to the ground, but they quickly got back up to their feet.

"It came from inside," Lucan said.

Cato nodded as they raced toward the back door. They had the best chance of getting in there before any of the other hybrids. It would all rest on them to make sure things were handled.

"The townspeople are the waitstaff!" he shouted to them as they entered. "Get as many out as you can."

The military had screened all the employees, but military screening wouldn't mean shit if their enemy were using their mind-control signal, which they'd done a good job of refining in recent months.

Even if the townspeople were dangerous, they were just as much pawns in the game as anyone else. Poor mind-controlled bastards. From what the hybrids had seen, some of them even had to deal with the horror of realizing the evil they were doing during a mind-control session, but were helpless to stop it.

And for that matter, it might only be a single person in the whole group who was involved in the attack. The rest were just innocent people trying to earn a living.

"Leah," Alair said quietly.

Cato's first thoughts were of Wendy, but he had to trust that she would be all right. She was trained for combat. Wendy would be fine. She had to be.

Red lights flashed as they raced through the kitchen. Nikon stayed behind to help pull the staff outside to safety. Many people rested against the wall or lay on the ground, dazed and couching.

Water from sprinklers rained down on them and didn't help with the traction on the floor, but Cato pushed through. It was better they sprinklers did their job than people died from a fire.

Shouts and screams sounded from the ballroom. The sounds sent chills to his bones.

He fought to keep his emotions under control as he and Alair stepped into the room. Smoke, water, and debris made it hard to see far in front of them, even with their keen sight.

Chaos reigned. The explosion had ripped a corner completely from the room. Red stains streaked the walls around them, and he tried not the think who had been near when it had gone off. That was no way to die.

In the middle of it all, he spotted Wendy and Colonel Hall shouting orders to the soldiers they came across. The men and women may have been at a party, but they were still members of the Army, and knew their way around tense situations.

The were concentrating on trying to clear out the windows and free people trapped under debris.

He nodded to Alair and then both sprinted to separate rubble piles, yanking wood and metal off trapped people and hybrids.

"Damn cowardly bombing bastards," Cato growled as he freed two trapped soldiers and helped them up.

Rubble covered the closest door leading outside. They were having to send people through the halls, which caused its own issues.

As he took in more of the horror, a man nearby caught his eye. The vacant stare that met his made his blood run cold. It was one of them. He was sure of it.

"Wait," he shouted to the man.

Cato ran toward the open door the man was slipping through. Maybe he could get to the bomb before it went off.

The man raised something in his hand, some sort of trigger.

"Shit," Cato said. He slammed the door shut. A thunderous boom shook the other side. Another explosion burst from another part of the room.

The combined force slammed into Cato and sent him flying from the scene. The heavy metal door slammed into him as he fell hard to the ground. The wall crumbled around the empty hole.

He'd saved the people in the room, but that did little for the fire and structural damage. If they didn't get out of there, the building would collapse and kill them anyway.

"Cato!" Wendy shouted over the carnage around him.

His mind focused on her voice as he forced himself back from nearly passing out.

He lifted the door off and grunted when he sat up. Nothing he couldn't recover from.

"Man up, Cato," Colonel Hall shouted down at him.

Cato wanted to laugh, but damned if she wasn't right. There wasn't any time to waste. If they were going to get out of there, he needed to get up. Moving was everything.

Wendy wrapped her arms around him. "Thank God you're safe."

CHAPTER NINETEEN

WENDY KNEW they didn't have time for her to hug him, but she couldn't stop. She had been so worried since the explosion. It had come from nowhere when the bomb went off. The sound deafened her and threw her off balance.

Immediately, Colonel Hall swung into action telling the men to start clearing out the wounded and seeing to those that were able to move. She'd dealt with this sort of situation before in Afghanistan.

Wendy stood, and all her training kicked in. She knew she couldn't think about if Cato was alive. All she could do was focus on the people in front of her and keep them alive.

When he'd entered the room, a sigh of relief slipped out. She'd never been so relieved to see another person.

Even now, battered by the latest explosion, he was still alive. His warm body pressed to her own.

She glanced over to the floor nearby. Leah sat with Jamie's head in her lap. Jamie was still unconscious from the first explosion. They'd had to dig her out, and Wendy worried for her friend, though she was still breathing.

"Sergeant," Colonel Hall said sharply. "We need to move."

Wendy pulled back from Cato and helped him to his feet. His hand was firmly in hers as they made their way toward the others.

She could see several casualties lying dead on the floor. Both hybrids and humans had been unable to escape the first explosion. The attack was too sudden.

Alair and a hybrid she'd didn't know were pulling the rubble away from the door that led directly outside. They had been sealed in. The hall was closed off now, and the second explosion had closed off the way the hybrids had come.

The other hybrid looked over at Cato. "You okay?"

"Well enough, Lucan," Cato said.

Lucan? Something about that name rang a bell, but Wendy set it to the side for a moment. She didn't have time to worry about it.

"Nikon is on the other side," Lucan shouted. "If we can make enough room, we might be able to squeeze some of them out."

Cato nodded. Wendy watched as he grimaced in pain from his injuries but still pulled the heavy blocks away.

Groaning and creaking sounded from the building now. She wondered just how long it was before the entire thing collapsed. Too many load-bearing walls and supports had been destroyed.

The only thing they had going for them was that the sprinklers had stopped, making things a bit less slick, but she worried that was from damage. The situation didn't look good in general.

"Lucan, can you pull the last piece aside?" Cato said.

Lucan climbed up to the top of the pile with ease and wedged a large piece of the wall against another, creating enough space to get through.

She breathed in the cool night air, glad to have the fresh breeze.

"I'll take the injured woman," Lucan said.

Cato nodded. He lifted Jamie carefully and handed her to the other hybrid.

Lucan disappeared to the other side.

"Colonel," Cato turned to the commander.

Colonel Hall frowned at him and shook her head. "Like hell I'm going before my people are out," she said firmly. "First Leah, and then Sergeant Morris."

"Are you okay?"

It was Leah's quiet voice that made the group turn. A

woman walked toward them. Her head hung low, hair shadowing her face.

"Stay away from her," Cato said with a growl. "She's one of the suicide bombers."

Wendy stared hard at the woman. She looked just like anyone else. Nothing to make her stand out. She didn't even have anything strapped to her chest.

How could she be a suicide bomber? After a moment, she realized the woman had some sort of trigger in her hand.

The girl stopped not far from Leah and stared directly at her. Her face was contorted in pain, tears dripping down her face.

"Run," she whispered. "Run."

Wendy felt a rush of air as someone breezed past her. Alair.

He pushed Leah back and turned to where they were. "Get them out," he shouted.

"Alair!"

Wendy turned to see Nikon at the opening just before Cato's warm arms gripped her waist. His warmth enveloped her, making things seem, just for a moment, like they might be all right.

"Get Leah," Cato shouted to Nikon. "Hang on, Colonel."

Wendy gasped as another explosion tore through the room. Her surroundings blurred as Cato knocked some falling debris away from her. The chunk of wood sliced his cheek. He deposited her on the soft grass and then rushed back for the colonel.

Several seconds passed. Maybe minutes. She couldn't be sure.

Someone was screaming, and she wasn't so sure it wasn't her, but she didn't want to open her eyes to check. Didn't want to see what was left of the man that had saved her friend.

Cool air hit her face, and she breathed in deep breaths to

keep down the bile.

She finally opened her eyes, breathing slowly.

The rest of the building collapsed, fire consuming it and a column of smoke rising into the sky.

Nikon and Leah sat in the grass. Her face was buried against his chest as she sobbed loudly. On the other side of Cato, Colonel Hall sat on her knees. Her head was bleeding from their quick retreat.

Soot covered Cato. Blood dripped from his face, arm, and side. His shirt had been scorched. Despite his stoic demeanor, she could see the pain in his tight expression, both physical and emotional.

Wendy placed her head against the man next to her and let the tears fall until she no longer had the strength to cry.

CHAPTER TWENTY

THE LIGHTS STILL FLASHED OUTSIDE the office building, but Cato had grown accustomed to them now. It had been several hours since they had escaped the destroyed ballroom, but it felt like no time at all. Over and over, the scene played in his head.

Alair was gone. The kind man who had been like a brother to him had behaved exactly like his true nature: selflessly.

It had nearly killed Cato to see Nikon as he sat there in the grass with Leah, both of their hearts broken by the same loss.

Cato now sat on the couch in Titus's office with Wendy pressed against his side and squeezing his arm if he moved at all. She hadn't spoken more than a few words since they had gotten out.

"I should have evacuated the second you mentioned the bomb threat," Colonel Hall said. "How many dead?"

Titus sighed. "Three hybrids and five soldiers."

The colonel nodded to Titus. "It would have been more if it weren't for your men."

Cato raised a brow. He wasn't expecting that considering how things had been since the military had stepped in.

"You could have just worried about your people, but I saw true bravery today," she said quietly. "Your men chose to protect my people at their own risk. This goes against all the reports that have landed on my desk."

Titus nodded. "I'm not surprised," he said. "I think there are some that want to see us used for other purposes."

Colonel Hall leaned against the desk.

"You said this was our government," she said, her eyes

narrowed. "If my government, even if it's just a faction, has turned against me, I'd like to know."

Titus nodded. "We don't have solid proof, but we have a lot of evidence that leads us to believe that might be the case."

"Unfortunately, without proof, that makes it hard to start a case," she said. "How many families are here now? Children?"

Titus glanced over to Cato. He wasn't sure where this conversation was going. "About a dozen families and over a dozen children."

She sighed loudly. "I never thought I'd see the day when my government would bomb our own country. I swore to defend the people of this country from enemies both foreign and domestic." She glanced between the hybrids in the room. "Take them and go. Get out of here before these bastards try something again. I'm not going to be a party to the murder of families. At least we can get them out of here until we get this situation under control."

"And if you don't?" Titus said.

"Then maybe everyone will just have to… evacuate and get lost along the way. For now though, families and children."

Wendy stiffened next to Cato and stood. "Ma'am? What about orders?"

The colonel smiled at her. "This is a war zone. We weren't told what we were walking into. I can't guarantee their safety here." She slammed a fist on the desk. "I'm not going to stay here as some bastard hiding in some office in DC hires some crazies to bomb us." Her eyes widened. "They killed innocent people, and they killed men under my command!" She took a deep breath. "I was told to protect the hybrids, and that's exactly what I'm doing. Even if that means letting them leave."

Cato stood next to Wendy. "This is my home," he said firmly.

The colonel raised a brow. "Your home is a dangerous place. If they are willing to go this far, who knows what they'll try next time?"

Cato shrugged and looked over to the woman standing next to him. "This is where I belong."

The colonel glanced over at Titus. He nodded at Cato.

"You've got a place to go I presume," she said to Titus. "I know you have something up your sleeve."

Titus laughed. "They said you were smart."

The colonel gave him a genuine smile. "A good leader always has a backup plan and a way to extract the troops." She eyed him. "One of the hybrids that helped tonight was named Lucan."

Titus quirked a brow. "Yes?"

"I recognized the name. He's supposed to be dead."

"Sometimes it's good to have resources no one knows about."

The colonel nodded. "You're even sneakier than I thought, good thing sometimes in a leader. I want to do what I can to help you. I'd like to help you all leave, but there's no way I can manage it with the current situation."

Titus nodded. "Thank you," he said quietly. "We'll take the families and children for now. This is no place for any of them."

"You should go tonight before we've got every agency crawling up our ass," she said. "Sergeant, I'd like a word."

Wendy looked up into his eyes and then gave a small squeeze before following the colonel out.

"She's a good woman," Titus said.

Cato turned and nodded. He wasn't sure which woman he was talking about, but the description fit both.

"You weren't wrong," Titus said and sat down on the chair. "This is our home. There are many others who want to stay and fight with you. To help pave a world where human and hybrid can live in peace."

Cato was slightly surprised. He hadn't realized that there were others that felt the same way.

"And I'm never going to ask a hybrid to leave his Vestal," Titus said. "You can be happy with her and still help our people."

Cato nodded and then thought back to the initial warning. Their enemy was always one step ahead of them. "Jill Hope wasn't clear about who was involved."

"She has an anonymous tipster who definitely said the government was involved, but that it might not be Senator Woods."

"Huh."

"That changes nothing for now. You'll do your part here, and the families and children will move to the new facility."

Cato nodded

"I'm going with my family," Titus said. "They need me at the new facility."

It made sense, but he still couldn't help but be surprised by it. "Who will be the leader then?"

Titus smiled at him, and he could see just how tired he was. "You."

Panic rose up in his chest. "Me? What the hell do I know about being a leader?"

Titus chuckled. "You know more than I did coming into the title." He stood and clapped Cato on the shoulders. "You are a leader," he said. "It's in your very blood. It's why you spend so much of your time alone and why you question every move that is made. You were made to do this job."

Had this been his plan all along?

"Wendy…"

Titus nodded. "A strong leader needs a strong woman," he said. "She is exactly that."

He felt it as well. The strength that Wendy brought about in him.

"Thank you, sir," he said quietly.

Titus smiled. "Have faith in yourself. I do."

* * *

Wendy stood outside taking in deep breaths as she stared at the red lights flashing down the road. It seemed so surreal.

A heavy arm wrapped around her, and she knew without even looking that it was Cato. Just having him near her brought a comfort.

She'd feared he would leave with the others. Hearing him say he would stay gave her the emotional strength she needed to continue.

"You okay?" he asked quietly.

Wendy turned to look at him in the night. "No," she whispered.

He nodded. "He was a good man," Cato said.

She sighed and leaned her head against his chest. His arm tightened around her.

"What did the colonel have to say?" he asked.

Wendy turned her head towards his. Their faces were much closer together now. "That she was wrong. Life is short and to live every day that way."

Cato leaned down and kissed her. It was soft and comforting. She could feel the strength from it reach into her very soul and pull her back from the darkness there.

When he pulled away, she continued to stare up at him. "So what now?"

He placed his forehead against hers and breathed in deeply. "We stay," he said. "We protect the people we care about, and we make a life."

Wendy turned and wrapped her arms around him. "I thought you had died," she whispered. "I thought you had died, and that I'd never get to tell you how much I love you."

Cato pulled her in even closer. His mouth against her ear. "My life was darkness without you," he whispered. "You are my heart. I love you, now and forever."

Wendy kissed him again with all the love she felt in her heart. They would stay, and they would live the life that others weren't able to. They would create a new path in life, and they would spend their days sharing the love they had for one another. From now until forever.

A Note from Madison

Thank you for reading *Cato*. If you enjoyed this book, please consider reviewing it. We authors live and die by reviews.

Please keep an eye out for the next book in the series, *Lucan*.

You can join my mailing list at **http://eepurl.com/OX9r5**

Luna Lodge: Hunters of Atlas (Paranormal Romance)

Magnus (Hunters #1)
Nero (Hunters #2)
Lucas (Hunters #3)
Sergius (Hunters #4)
Marcus (Hunters #5)
Jace (Hunters #6)

Shadow Series

Shadow's Embrace (Shadow #1)

Special Forces

Trent (Special Forces #1)
Johnny (Special Forces #2)

Road House (Contemporary Romance Short Stories)

Letting Go (Road House #1)
Holding On (Road House #2)
Standing By (Road House #3)

Privileged (New Adult Romance)

Privileged (Privileged #1)
Elite (Privileged #2)

Author Bio

Madison currently lives with her husband and two children in the Valley of the Sun in Arizona. After leaving the frozen tundra of the north, she was more surprised than anyone with how much she has enjoyed living in the desert. Seeing as she stated on more than one occasion before moving to Arizona how much she hated heat, it was an odd move, but it seems her hatred for sub-zero temperatures and ice has won out in the end.

When she's not writing, she's enjoying time with her family. Madison and her family frequent festivals in the area, as well as local cultural events, and spend time with family in the area. In the summer, she is most likely to be found in the pool with the family and in the winter by the fireplace. Since both her children are autistic, days can be a little chaotic, but with her husband beside her, there's nothing she can't handle.

Her webpage is **http://madisonstevensauthor.com/**

She can be contacted at madisonstevensauthor@gmail.com

69848987R00073

Made in the USA
Columbia, SC
24 April 2017